PRASE FOR CODE NAME  s

Mission 1: Operation Rubber S...   th a
multi-dimensional protagonist th   ced,
well choreographed action and bits ɔ...ɔ...

"Like *Harry Potter*, this YA series is fun for kids of all ages!"—Tawni Waters, Author, *Beauty of the Broken; Siren Song; Top Travel Writers of 2010*

"I'm 50 years older than the target market for this book, and I couldn't put it down!"—George Nolly, Airline Pilot, Author, *Hamfist* trilogy

Mission 2: Cartel Kidnapping—"**4/4 STARS!** Fast-paced, action-packed, and well developed. Auxier grabs the reader. Reluctant and avid readers who enjoy teenage fast-paced spy adventures will love reading this book!"—*Online Book Club*

Mission 3: Jihadi Hijacking—"**4/4 STARS!** Superb on so many levels. A well-executed juggling act with just the right amount of humor. A highly detailed, entertaining, and character-driven spy thriller!"—*Online Book Club*

"An engaging espionage tale that aims to enlighten readers!"—*Kirkus Review*

Mission 4: Yakuza Dynasty—"**4/4 STARS!**—ONE OF THE BEST BOOKS I'VE EVER READ! More twists and turns than many mysteries. Amazing that this level of action, intrigue and humor could last an entire book. Absolutely in the same league as the Harry Potter series!"—*Online Book Club Official Review*

PRAISE FOR *THE LAST BUSH PILOTS*
"TOP 100, BREAKTHROUGH NOVELS, 2013!"—Amazon.com

"You won't put it down while the midnight sun still shines!"—*Airways* Magazine

"Suspense and drama in spades. Romantic entanglements and a covert mission help this aviation tale take off!"—Kirkus Reviews

"Eric Auxier is the next Tom Clancy of aviation!"—Tawni Waters, Author, *Beauty of the Broken*; *Siren Song*; *Top Travel Writers 2010*

"I flew through *The Last Bush Pilots* in one sitting, keeping my seatbelt securely fastened!"—John Wegg, Editor, *Airways* Magazine

PRAISE FOR *There I Wuz! Adventures from 3 Decades in the Sky-Volumes 1-3*
"When we come across an aviator with a gift for storytelling, those adventures jump off the page. Eric Auxier is such an author, and *There I Wuz!* is the book."
—Karlene Petitt, Airline Pilot; CNN Correspondent; Author, *Flight to Success*

"I freaking love this series!"—Steve Thorne, pilot-videographer, flightchops.com

"An entertaining peek at the highlights—and sometimes lowlights—of military and commercial pilots who've been-there-done-that."—Ron Rapp, pilot-writer, rapp.org

"Captain Eric Auxier is not just a pilot, he is an aviation author, ambassador and legend. He opens the bullet-proof cockpit door and welcomes us into the most technically-advanced, risk-laden, yet safest profession."—Captain Richard de Crespigny, author, *QF32*

This is a work of fiction. All of the characters, organizations, places and events portrayed in this novel are either products of the author's imagination or are used fictionally.

Code Name: Dodger Mission 1—Operation Rubber Soul
Copyright © 2009 by Eric B. Auxier
Cover image copyright 2010 by Eric B. Auxier. All rights reserved.

Mission 2: Cartel Kidnapping
Copyright © 2014 by Eric B. Auxier
Cover image copyright 2014 by Eric B. Auxier. All rights reserved.

Mission 3: Jihadi Hijacking
Copyright © 2015 by Eric B. Auxier
Cover image copyright 2015 by Eric B. Auxier. All rights reserved.

Mission 4: Yakuza Dynasty
Copyright © 2016 by Eric B. Auxier
Cover image copyright 2016 by Eric B. Auxier. All rights reserved.

Published by EALiterary Press, Phoenix, AZ
Printed in the United States of America

EALiterary Press ebook edition 2016
EALiterary Press paperback edition 2016

CONTACT INFO:
> BOOK WEBSITE: cndodger.com
> CONTACT AUTHOR: eric@capnaux.com
> AUTHOR BLOG: capnaux.com

The Code Name: Dodger series is available for purchase in print or ebook at amazon.com/author/ericauxier

Special request by the Author:
Please leave an honest rating and review of this book, to help others decide whether to read it! U.S. Amazon Link: amazon.com/author/ericauxier

GOT EBOOK?
If you purchased this book via amazon, get the ebook for free!

A portion of proceeds from the author's other works go to the international orphan relief funds, flyingkitesglobal.org and Warmblankets.org

ISBN-13: 978-1479113675
ISBN-10: 1479113670

CODE NAME:

DODGER

OPERATION RUBBER SOUL

A NOVEL BY:

ERIC AUXIER

FOR MOM AND DAD

TABLE OF CONTENTS

CODE NAME: DODGER

ERIC AUXIER

PROLOGUE: FLASH TRAFFIC

CENTRAL INTELLIGENCE AGENCY
LANGLEY, VIRGINIA

* *TOP SECRET—EYES ONLY—EXTREMELY URGENT* *

TO: KING COLE/CIA HQ
FR: AGENT FAGIN
LOC: NORTH BROOKLYN, NY
RE: ENEMY AGENT PHARAOH
OP: RUBBER SOUL

DISCOVERED ENEMY AGENT PHARAOH'S TARGET:
REED, JUSTIN M; TEEN ORPHAN

ENEMY AGENT OBJCTV: REMAINS UNKN.
ENEMY AGENT IDENT: REMAINS UNKN.

END MSG.

CHAPTER 1: STRANGERS LURKING

"Justin, don't look now, but there's some freakazoid watchin' us."

I fought off the urge to peek. "Cop?" I asked.

Randy ran his long black fingers through his shoulder length dreadlocks, then shook his head. "Nah, at least not a local. I think he's a perv."

Spinning a three-sixty on my skateboard, I spied the stranger. Hunched over and scrawny, the guy hid behind dark shades, gangster hat and a big black trench coat, like secret agents wear in the movies. All I could see of his face was this ugly scar that creased the left side of his neck and cheek.

"New York's finest," I mumbled.

We skated around the basketball court in front of the orphanage for a few more minutes, and finally figured out who he was watching. Me.

Randy slapped a hand across my shoulder and snickered. "I think he likes cute little fourteen year-old white boys like you, Justin."

I shoved him away. "Get outta here, you skank."

Doug joined us. "What's up?"

I nodded behind me. "Scarface over there's scoping on us."

Blowing away a lock of black hair from his dark brown eyes, he glanced sideways at the guy. Doug looked a lot like me, a white boy but with dark features. Except his looks come from Italian blood. Mine come from Mom, who was half Japanese. I've got a bit of almond shape to my eyes, but usually people can't tell. I had Mom's hair too, long, straight, shoulder-length and jet black.

"Let's see who he is," Doug suggested. "I'll pick his pocket."

Randy sneered. "You couldn't pick a nose. I'll do it."

We devised a plan.

I kept skating, spinning 360s and stuff while Randy and Doug slipped out of the fenced courtyard and onto the sidewalk. They approached him from opposite sides, Randy on foot, Doug on skateboard. As he neared, Doug pretended to trip up on a crack in the sidewalk and fall into Scarface. At that instant, Randy strode by and swiftly lifted the guy's wallet from behind.

"Oh, sorry, man," Doug said.

"Watch it, kid, or you'll be wearin' that skateboard around your neck," Scarface hissed, angrily brushing at his coat.

"Said I was sorry, smeghead."

Randy walked on as if nothing had happened. He flashed me a thumbs-up. Mission accomplished.

I smiled. Randy was a pro pickpocket. And a great teacher at it, too.

See, I used to be pretty dumb. As an Air Force brat, I'd lived all over the world, even learned Spanish and Japanese, but I'd never lived on the street.

Then Dad was murdered.

It was just a couple years ago. Mom had already died in a drowning accident back when I was six, so they sent me here, to the North Brooklyn Juvenile Home. I arrived a cocky young kid, but not very *street* smart. Randy all changed that. He taught me the ways of the asphalt jungle, including how to pick pockets and locks like the gangs do.

Randy wasn't a gangbanger, but an older guy he knew was. The loser kept trying to lure Randy into his gang by teaching us stuff like street fighting, hot wiring cars, even hacking computers. Me, I pride myself on being independent like my dad had been, and not a mindless zombie for some whacked-out drug dealer. So I talked Randy out of joining. But we still got some good training out of it. We'd even stole from the guy a couple lock pick sets made up to look like Swiss Army knives. After several months' practice, there wasn't an orphanage lock or computer we couldn't crack.

Those skills paid off whenever we ran away, which was about every other month. The last time we tried, Randy got caught right away. I got pretty far though, six weeks down the road, and almost to L.A.

They'd shipped me back to the orphanage only two days ago and now this. Some New York nutbag staring at me in broad daylight.

We skated inside and ran up to our third floor dorm room. Doug and I knelt beside Randy's bunk as he belly-flopped onto the bed. A few other orphans joined us, curious. Randy smiled up at me. He dangled Scarface's wallet like it was a prize fish. I grabbed for it but he jerked it away.

"Unh-uh, Mr. Reed, its my catch. I gets to open it." He did. He spread the leather flaps of the billfold wide, and we peered in. I scrunched my forehead in confusion. Except for a few bucks, the wallet was empty. No credit cards, no driver's license, no I.D. of any kind.

Randy snatched the bills and tossed me the empty wallet. "Here, you get the leftovers."

I frowned. "Thanks a lot."

Doug said, "Hey, man, this is too weird. We'd better take this to Kraut."

"No way," Randy and I chorused. Kraut was Mrs. Bertha Kraumas, the head of our orphanage. One of the main reasons we kept running away.

"She'd panic and keep me confined to quarters for life," I said.

"*And* call the cops," Randy added.

"I've had enough of them for awhile," I said with a nervous laugh.

Doug bent close across the bed as if he had a secret to share. "Speaking of cops, somethin's up in there," he whispered. His eyes darted right and left.

"What do you mean?" I asked, glad for the distraction from the no-name freak.

"Some guy's been in Kraut's office all morning. Gotta be a cop."

I gulped and looked at Randy. He just sat back and rolled his eyes. "He's probably her sex slave." Everyone snickered.

"Ooh gross," Doug said, crinkling his nose and pointing his finger down his throat as if barfing.

I laughed too, but the thought of a cop talking to Kraut worried me.

Doug turned serious. "I mean it, guys. I'll bet he's Department of Corrections. Checking up on you and Randy, and that brilliant escape you two made. Jeez, I can't believe you guys. Stealing the school bus in the middle of the night and going on a three-state joy ride! How'd you get so far without getting caught, anyway, Justin?"

"If I knew that, I'd tell you," I said, dodging his question.

Actually, I was lucky. And I relied on some tricks Dad had taught me. See, after he left the Air Force, he got this job as a prison guard at Attica. He used to have all these great stories about prison breaks. But the last one cost him his life.

A convict shot him. The killer's name was burned into my memory like a brand: Sly Barett. The day Dad died, I swore that I would somehow find Sly and get revenge. The cops never did catch the scumbag, so I figured it was up to me.

Doug shook his head. "Kraut says Randy's gettin' sent upriver to juvenile prison for sure. And I'll bet you're right behind him, Justin."

Randy jabbed a finger at Doug. "Hey, I got news for you, pal. No one's going to Juvy. There ain't even any charges pressed yet, anyways." He snickered. "What would they call it, anyway, Grand Theft School Bus?" We laughed.

"So, Justin, have you seen Sherry yet?" Doug asked.

I shook my head.

"She's been asking about you," he teased in a singsong voice.

"I'd like to see her one last time before I leave."

Doug's eyes widened. "Hey, you're not going nowhere. They wouldn't *really* send you to Juvy. Would they?"

"Who said anything about that? I'm splitting before they have the chance."

Randy brightened and stared wickedly back. "Where to this time, Justin? Can't be L.A. They'd expect us there."

I fiddled with the empty wallet and stared off into space. "Well, I've always wanted to see London."

"Oh, but of course," Randy said in a fake British accent, holding his pinky out like an old lady drinking tea. "Be one of them prissy, upper class English orphans like that Oliver loser."

I shrugged and smiled. The kids always joked about my ragged copy of *Oliver Twist*. I read it when traveling. Dad gave it to me, right before he died. Afterwards I sort of felt like I was Oliver, the poor orphan that always got the shaft from life.

Like when I got dumped off at the orphanage for the first time. I'd always been small and scrawny for my age, and when I walked through the doors, Randy and the others surrounded me. Randy started shoving me around, calling me a punkass little white boy.

I knew from Dad's prison stories that, to earn their respect, a new inmate had to stand up to the biggest one or suffer the consequences. And that was Randy. So, timing his moves, I grabbed his wrist and neck and Judo flipped him onto the floor, smacking his head good. Doug took a step forward, but my eyes drilled into him and he thought the better of it. As Randy bounded up, I raised my fists. But to my surprise, he grinned wide and gave me a great big bear hug. "Welcome to your new home, kid," he exclaimed. "You'll do *juust* fine here." After that, we'd always been inseparable.

Shaking away the memory, I looked back down in time to see Randy pull out a cellphone from his back pocket. It was one of the latest gizmos I'd never seen before, all slick and fancy. My jaw dropped.

"Hey, where'd you get—" I started.

"You think I was gonna let the man skate with his sweet phone?" he bragged, tapping the touchscreen. "I can get a good price for this baby, my friend."

I laughed. "Randy, you could steal the panties off a Victoria's Secret model!"

"Hehe. Who says I ain't already?"

He eyed it closer. "Looks similar to an older model iPhone. But it's brand new." His leer turned into a frown. "Hmm. No markings on it, anywhere. No manufacturer, no serial number, no name." He tapped the unlock screen harder. He blinked. "Hey, something's wrong with this thing. It don't —"

"Invalid biometrics and DNA scan," the phone spoke in a stern lady's voice, *"Central database access denied."*

Our mouths dropped open. On the screen, a light blue box surrounded flashing red images of a thumbprint, eyeball and a spinning schematic of a DNA double helix.

"What the hell's a biometrics and DNA scan?" Doug asked.

"What the hell's a central database?" Randy wondered aloud.

Though none of us orphans had ever had our own phones, we'd certainly seen our share of the latest rich boy toys as they passed from our light fingers and into those of Randy's gangster fences. And a talking phone with a DNA scan, we all knew, was *not* the latest craze.

We stared at each other in disbelief. "Some iPhone."

"More like, *spy*Phone," I said in awe.

"Cop," Doug repeated. "Gotta be with that guy in Kraut's office."

"N-no man," Randy replied. "This ain't no cop. Somethin' heavier. Way heavier."

"What's . . . what's heavier than . . . ." my thoughts raced.

"Hey, Reed, gimme that wallet again." I handed it to him. Squinting, Randy felt around the inside of the wallet. "Hey," he announced, "there's a slit in the lining . . . ." Randy dug into it and came up with a photo. A photo of me.

I gasped.

Randy read aloud a note scribbled the back. "Subject: Justice Malcomb Reed, nickname Justin. Location: N. Brooklyn Juvenile Home. Item: Gold Master key, number p1505." Randy looked sharply at me.

My hands trembled. "Wha—what's going on? What's it mean?"

Randy held the note up. "It means somebody wants something from you, but he don't want nobody to know who he is. *That's* why no I.D."

"What's that part about a key?" Doug asked. The two looked at me.

I shrugged. "I don't have any key. I don't know what it means. Unless . . . ."

"Unless what?" Randy pressed.

"Nothing."

I remembered the investigation of Dad's murder. A couple real creepy detectives with sunglasses and trench coats searched our apartment the very day it happened. They tore our place apart, then asked me about some kind of key. But I didn't have it, whatever it was. Maybe now Sly Barett had found me and was after it—after *me*. I shivered at the thought.

The dorm room speaker crackled. I jumped.

"Justice Malcomb Reed, you're wanted in Director Kraumas' office," the secretary's nasally voice announced over the intercom. She said my full name, as if there were a ton of kids named Justice in the dorm. "Justice Malcomb Reed, to the Director's office immediately."

"Uh-oh, here it comes." Being called to Kraut's office was like being sentenced to the gas chamber. But at least it distracted me from Scarface and Sly and the key.

Randy patted my shoulder. "Hang in there, Juh-*stice*," he teased. Normally I would've punched him out for calling me that, but other things occupied my mind.

"Go get 'er, killer," offered Doug.

I trudged down the long corridor between cots, everyone's eyes heavy on me. Some boys slapped me on the back or punched my arm reassuringly. Others just nodded. I swung the double doors open and shuffled downstairs.

Standing in front of her big oak door and ready to knock, I froze. Maybe Scarface was a cop. Maybe he was in with her right now, handcuffs twirling, ready to slap them on me the moment I stepped in. I glanced about. No one around. I could disappear right now, I thought, and never have to face Kraut's sentence. I sighed. No, I had to take my punishment. One thing Dad had taught me, you couldn't run from yourself. I sucked in a deep breath and knocked softly.

"M-Mrs. Kraumas?" I whispered, hoping she wouldn't hear. But she always had sonar ears and radar eyes.

"Enter," she barked, her booming voice easily penetrating the heavy door. I twisted the big brass knob and heaved the door open a crack. "Come in." I hesitated. "*Now*," I scooted in. "Close it behind you, Justice."

Whenever she gets really pissed she calls me Justice.

She read some papers in my file while I stood on the carpet, sweating. She leaned back in her seat, still reading, her eyes narrowed. I always wondered how come that chair never collapsed under her huge bag of fat. She looked up at me and spoke.

"You're like a tornado, Justice. You leave a path of destruction a mile wide. I don't even know where to begin." She shuffled through the papers. "Pickpocketing our bus driver, stealing his *bus*, for heaven's sake. Interstate transport of a stolen vehicle . . . ."

"I, um—"

"Silence. You're safe on those. Randy confessed to all counts. Claims you weren't even on the bus. Says it was he alone. And he'll pay dearly for it, I assure you." She peered up at me from her bifocals. "But I've no doubt you had a hand in it, too."

I breathed an inward sigh of relief. I couldn't believe Randy had taken the entire rap. I was the one who'd lifted the guy's keys. All Randy did was drive us away. I couldn't let him take the fall alone. I opened my mouth to confess, but Kraut cut me off.

"Continued truancy. I'm tired of hearing that. You still are underage, in case you forgot. Illegal employment for a minor, pockets picked and other apparent thefts along the way, all having *your* distinct earmark." She stopped suddenly, frowned, and threw the papers on the desk. "Frankly, I'm relieved when you set out on these adventures. Keeps the trouble around here to a minimum. But it all comes to a head when you return."

She looked up at me. "Why do you want to leave so awfully bad, anyway, Mr. Reed? You get three square meals a day, a decent education, an occasional field trip."

"Well, my parents, they're buried in Los Angeles, and I just—"

"Forget it," she said with a wave of her hand. She tossed her specs on the desk, leaned on her elbows and rubbed her eyes. She paused and looked up from between her wrinkled hands. "Randy's as good as gone. He'll get a fair trial, then off to juvenile prison. I was worried about how I was going to keep you out of the secure center, too. But it seems our problem has solved itself. *Conditionally*, that is."

I raised my eyebrows at that. "Yes?"

"I got a phone call early today. Local Department of Justice. Some bigwig. He said all charges would be dropped against you—"

"All right!" I shook my fists in triumph. "I always knew a department named 'Justice' couldn't be all bad. Both of us go free? Me and Randy?"

She frowned. "No. Just you. *If* you concede to a . . . a psychological experiment."

I cocked my head. "What kind of 'psychological experiment'?"

She nodded to the back of the room. "This gentleman will explain."

I wheeled in surprise. There, on her couch in the back of the room, sat a stranger I hadn't noticed before. He looked old, at least late 30s, and thin. Definitely in shape though. His fancy suit and tie, crew cut and clean shaven face made me think FBI. And that made me nervous.

"Justice Malcomb Reed, meet Dr. Robert Cheney," she said.

He stood and offered his hand. I didn't take it. Instead I crossed my arms and scowled.

"Who's he?" I demanded in my toughest Brooklyn street voice. That usually makes a wannabe foster parent run for the hills. But he just chuckled like a king at a court jester and dropped his hand. I felt dumb.

"Where are your manners young man?" Kraut half shouted. "Dr. Cheney is a psychiatrist with the Department of Juvenile Corrections. He is particularly interested in your case, though for the life of me I don't know why. He's willing to take you under his wing to help, uh, *straighten* you out."

The doctor raised a palm up. "Now, now, Mrs. Kraumas, there's nothing wrong with Justice, so let's not get that in his head. He's merely missing some important things in his life. Right, Justice? May I call you Justice?"

"Justin. I hate the name 'Justice'," I said, glancing at Kraut.

"Okay, Justin. I will never call you by that other name again."

He sounded sincere. At least he seemed to respect me. We'd find out soon enough. Probably turn out to be some sadistic creep who liked to *play* with little boys. Well if that was the case, he'd get his teeth splattered with my fist.

He sat on the arm of Kraut's couch, something she *hates* when us kids do. Kraut frowned but said nothing. I couldn't help but snicker.

Dr. Cheney said, "Justin, I'm doing a case study on environmentally-challenged juveniles. I see from your files you've had quite a wide variety of life experiences. I think your profile would fit well into my experiment."

I narrowed my eyes. "Whaddya wanna do, hook up a bunch of computers to my brain and zap me or something?"

He laughed. "No, nothing so drastic. Just change your environment. Give you a home, personal care and attention. Give you things you always wanted but never had."

My mouth dropped open. Didn't sound too bad for a New York street kid. And he sure didn't act like all those other sappy adoption couples looking for a teenage teddy bear to hug.

He leaned forward. "What do you say?"

I stared at my shoes. "Sounds great, I guess."

"Good. How about I pick you up, say, tomorrow morning at eight a.m.?"

I shot a look at Kraut. "*Tomorrow?*"

She shrugged. "Yes, tomorrow." She leafed through another pile of documents on her desk. "Doctor, the process of transferring orphans usually takes weeks—*especially* for those with criminal charges pending," she added with a scowl and a glance my way. "But the papers are all here, in order."

Kraut was right. Moving orphans around took an endless mess of paperwork. To suddenly whip all the forms up at once was nothing short of a miracle. And, with the cops breathing down my neck, . . . no way in Halo.

Maybe she bought his story, but I didn't. Something fishy was going on. But I figured whatever scam this guy was pulling, I'd go along just to get out of this dump.

Kraut sighed and said, "I'm not sure who you know in Washington, Dr. Cheney, but I wish I had your pull with some of these other kids."

"Thank you, Mrs. Kraumas." He stood. "Well, its been a pleasure meeting you, both of you." He gathered up his trench coat. Suddenly I noticed the cellphone on his hip. The exact model that Scarface had outside. I sucked in my breath.

The doctor looked at me and raised his brows. "Something wrong, Justin?"

"No," I whispered. I cleared my throat. "Um, did you come with anyone else today?"

"No. Why?"

"Oh. Some other guy outside had the same kind of coat and . . . and cell. Musta been a coincidence."

He stared at me for a long moment, his forehead wrinkled. "Yeah, coincidence," he said finally. "He shook Kraut's hand, then once again offered it to me. This time I took it. He smiled. "Tomorrow at eight, then."

"Eight," I mumbled, still shocked. He glided out.

With the doctor gone, I braced for Kraut's attack. She heaved herself out of the chair and leaned over her desk.

"You'd just better make this work, Justice," she snarled. "Behave, and he'll send you to L.A. But if you make me look bad, I'll take my pound of flesh out of your hide when they send you back here." She shook a finger at me. "I don't want to see you in this institution again. Not until you're much older and return to thank me for influencing you enough to keep your grades up."

That burned me good. I'd done it all for Dad. I swore I'd get to college somehow, like he always wanted me to.

She sat down hard. I winced as the rickety chair creaked with her weight. She bent back to her paperwork.

"This conversation is over," she announced. "Congratulations on your . . . *liberation*."

I stepped outside and closed the door. I leaned against it and breathed a huge sigh of relief. What a break. I really figured Juvy was next. And that's real prison.

L.A.

Moving to L.A. at last!

I walked back upstairs in a trance. As I swung the doors open to my floor, all conversation hushed, like when the bad guy enters the saloon in old black and white cowboy movies. I stumbled forward.

"Hey, Jus', you okay?" Randy asked, gently placing his hand on my back and guiding me forward.

"Looks like Kraut really pummeled him good this time," someone whispered.

"Here, you'd better sit down on my cot," Randy said. I did, then looked slowly up at him. Others gathered around, worried looks on their faces.

"I—I'm leaving," I whispered.

Randy jerked his head back in surprise. "Oh, no. To Juvy? What are you up for? Besides the usual, I mean?"

"Nothing. All charges dropped."

Randy's eyes lit up. "All charges dropped," he shouted. The room erupted in cheers. He slapped me on the back. "Right on. So where are you going?"

I looked at him. "L.A. After I do some psychology experiment."

He threw his head back and cackled. "Hey, everybody, Justin's gonna be a guinea pig in a *sy-ko-logie-kal* experiment!" The room erupted again, this time in laughter.

Somehow, I didn't feel like laughing.

CHAPTER 2: A SPY IN THE OINTMENT

After breakfast, I headed out front to meet Dr. Cheney. Wrapping my tattered leather flight jacket against the cool spring morning breeze, I grabbed my skateboard and slalomed down the cracked pavement to the gate, the third floor gang in tow. Randy carried my duffel bag, the one Dad used in the Air Force. He tossed it down at my feet.

"Will that be all, sir?" he asked, holding his palm out like a hotel porter expecting a tip.

I laughed and shoved him away. "Get lost, you leech." Then I looked him in the eyes. "Thanks for covering my butt on the charges, even if they did wind up dropping 'em all. I'm gonna pay you back, somehow. I promise."

He shrugged. "They was gonna bust me anyway. Better only one of us goes down. Think of it as my going away present. Keep in touch, man." Randy held out his hand, this time for a shake. I took it.

"I will."

A car roared up. My jaw dropped. Dr. Cheney screeched to the curb in a gleaming silver Corvette t-top, one of those new four seaters. Randy and I glanced at each other.

"No way," Randy said.

"You lucky scumbag," said Doug.

Cheney emerged from the car. He smiled and waved.

"Hey guys, how's it going?" he asked. We all just sort of nodded blankly. He came around to the curb and pointed to my duffel and board. "That all your gear?"

"Yep."

He tossed them into the back seat.

"Justin! Justin!" I turned to see Kraut waddling down the steps, tears streaming from her eyes. I couldn't believe it. She wrapped her flabby arms around me and squeezed till my eyes bugged out. Over her shoulder I saw the other kids snickering. I felt my cheeks burn with embarrassment. Pulling back, she held me at arms length. "I'll miss you so much, you little rascal."

"Yeah, uh, me too."

She sniffled. "I always knew you'd come out right. You're just too smart for this place."

"Uh, thanks," I stammered. I think Dr. Cheney sensed my less-than-enthusiastic feelings, as he opened the passenger door for me.

"Ready to go for a spin?"

"Yeah!"

"Hop in."

I did, then rolled the window down. Cheney got in the other side and fired up. I leaned over to him.

"Gun it," I whispered.

"Belt on?"

"Yeah."

"Okay. Cleared for takeoff!"

I sank deep into the bucket seat as he did the most perfect peel out ever. The tires screeched, the Vette fish-tailed and we left the gang in a cloud of blue tire smoke. I waved good-bye. Then turned to him.

"Great car, Dr. Chanley."

He laughed. "Its *Cheney*, not Chanely. But you can call me Bob."

"Okay, uh, Bob."

"And thanks. I've only had it a few weeks."

Playing with the dials to the digital satellite player, I said, "Wow, you must be loaded. Didn't know psychologists made so much."

"Psychiatrists."

"Whatever."

Once past the toll booth and out on the Jersey turnpike, he hit the throttle. Light poles whizzed by. Wind whipped my face. With the t-tops open it sounded like a jet. He zoomed past the other cars, zigzagging between lanes. I stuck my hands up like on a roller coaster, thrilled and a bit nervous at the high speed.

I felt free. Freer than I had since getting sent to the orphanage. No cops or Scarfaces after me. I could do anything, go anywhere. And I didn't have to worry about where my next meal was coming from.

"Say, lets grab a bite to eat. I'm starved," I said. I'd just eaten at the orphanage, but I felt like seeing where this guy would take me. Besides, I'm ready to eat, anytime, anywhere, despite my skin and bones.

"Lunch?" he asked. "You're on, pal. If you can wait a couple hours, we'll stop at a nice place I know." With an amused look, he eyed me. "Then we take you shopping for some new clothes. Get you out of those street rags."

I tugged proudly at my coat lapel. "Ain't nothin' wrong with my clothes. And my leather jacket might have that 'distressed' look, but its genuine Air Force issue."

He turned his attention back to the road. "Okay, jacket stays. But the rest goes."

"Deal." Then a funny thought hit me. "Say, where are we going, anyway? I don't even know where you work."

He laughed. "Wondered when you'd get around to that. I thought Mrs. Kraumas must've told you after I left yesterday."

"Kraut? Nah, she never says anything except, 'You're a rotten kid' or something. Besides, I don't much care, long as its far from the Home."

"Washington."

I jerked my head around and stared. "*D.C.*? All the way down there?"

"Yep. Ever been?"

I shook my head no.

"We're just west over the Potomac. In McLean, Virginia."

His phone warbled. He reached up and grabbed it from its charging cradle, mounted on the T-bar. A chill ran up my spine as he stuck his thumb in the middle of the screen. A thumbprint image flashed green. He held it to his ear.

"Cheney here." He glanced at me. "Just picked him up. Going to do some shopping first." He glanced at his watch. "E.T.A., fifteen hundred hours." He hung up. I looked questioningly at him. "The office," he explained. "E.T.A. means our Estimated Time of Arrival. You'll meet the others on my— uh, psych team then. Fifteen hundred hours means three p.m., military time."

I nodded. "Yeah, I know. Dad talked like that. 'Justin, be up at oh-five hundred hours for fishing duty'," I said in a husky voice. I turned back to Bob. "For a psychiatrist guy, you sure talk like a soldier."

He sighed big. "Soldiers. A lot of people think of us that way, actually." I was about to ask him what he meant by that, but he held up a hand. "No questions. I'll explain everything at the office, okay? So, you like fishing?"

I perked up. "Any time, anywhere. Dad and I used to go a lot, no matter where we lived. L.A., Japan, Panama, New York. That's what I miss most, I guess. Fishing. Fishing with Dad."

I gazed out the window and fought back a tear.

* * *

We ate at a place so fancy they probably served silver toothpicks afterward. If I was still living on the street, I could have dined in luxury on the leftovers sent to the garbage.

The waiter up front—Bob called him a *maitre d'*—looked up from his reservations book, wrung his hands submissively and practically slobbered all over Bob. The guy looked like a half-starved penguin in his fancy tuxedo.

"May I help you, sir?" he said in this nasally voice.

"Two for lunch."

Penguin almost fainted when he saw me standing behind Bob in my grubby street clothes. He bent back to his list.

"I'm afraid we're—" Bob waved a twenty under his nose. "Right this way, sir." Penguin snapped up the bill and led us away.

I couldn't believe it. What a scam. He took us to a table in the middle of the restaurant. The other snooty customers stared as we passed. Normally I would have felt real uncomfortable, but I was flying so high I just leered back at them till they returned to their own business.

At our table, a waiter almost sent me to the floor when he stuffed the chair under me.

"This ain't no McDonalds," I whispered to Bob across the gleaming, white-clothed table. I eyed the crystal glasses and real silverware lined up perfectly at our places. "Do you eat like this all the time?"

"No, just—" he paused as we were accosted by a team of waiters, two removing the extra silverware and stuff, and one asking for drink orders.

Bob said, "Whiskey sour, please. Justin?"

"Uh, no whiskey for me, thanks, too early," I snickered. "Um, Coke. No, Cherry Coke. Lots of ice. Oh, and a squirt of orange soda and a dash of root beer in it, too," I called after the waiter. I turned to Bob. "I could get used to this."

He chuckled. "As I was saying, I don't eat like this often. Only on special occasions."

The waitress came, a knockout blonde. When she smiled, I almost fainted. I could hardly concentrate on the menu she handed me, especially since it was all written in French. That's one language I'm clueless with.

Bob ordered for us both. In French.

Bob taught me the proper way to eat, too, with each piece of silverware and all that. I decided to go along with it. Whatever made him happy, I figured, so long as I was getting a free ride out of the deal. Besides, I got a kick from holding my pinky out and acting snobby. I think I blew Bob away when, for "dessert," I ordered a huge plate of sushi, then expertly attacked it with my chopsticks. Hadn't had it since Dad took me for my 11th birthday.

After lunch, we got back on I-95 south. Just north of Washington, we passed through Baltimore. I remembered my dad's best friend in the Air Force, Sgt. Carlos Martinez, lived in Baltimore. Dad, Carlos and I used to go fishing together outside Panama City. He taught me most of the Spanish I knew, especially the cuss words. After Dad's death, Carlos offered to adopt me, but I said no. He and his wife were pretty poor, and they already had four kids with another on the way, so an extra mouth to feed would've drained them.

"Say, can we stop in Baltimore and see an old friend of mine?" I asked.

He looked at me. "Sorry, no time. I've got a lot planned for you."

"Guess you're right." I gazed out the window. "I don't know if he even lives there anymore."

We spent the early afternoon shopping at a mall Bob said was close to work, and just down the street from his house.

Anything I wanted, he bought. Dad had been poor too, so we never had a shopping spree like this, except for maybe at the Salvation Army. After he quit the Air Force, Dad used to say that he had a big golden nest egg saved up for my college education, but I never saw it. When the will came out he had zilch. That was the only time I think he ever lied to me, saying he had tons of money already saved up. But I didn't mind. I figure he planned to scrimp the money from his prison job, and by the time I was old enough, he'd have it. So much for college.

"Hey, how 'bout this?" Bob held up to his waist a pair of ugly, plaid, neon green Bermuda shorts. Loud, obnoxious and rebellious, at one time it had been in style for skating. But not any more. I held my nose as if it stunk and waved it off.

He laughed and put it back on the rack. "Glad you have *some* taste."

After the shopping spree, Bob had me slip into my new suit and tie so I could be "presentable" to his staff. He knotted the tie for me. I couldn't help because, except for Dad's funeral, I'd never worn one before.

Once back on the Capital Beltway, he touched his thumb to the cell screen. "Call King Cole," he announced, holding the phone to his ear.

I snickered. What kind of name was that? I wondered. Nickname, I figured.

After a pause, he said into the receiver, "Shrink here. Yes sir, he's with me. On our way in now. E.T.A. twenty minutes." He hung up.

I looked at him and giggled. "'Shrink'?"

"That's slang for a psychiatrist," he explained. "It's also my code name."

A jolt ran down my spine. "C-code name? Whaddya mean by that? Like, like a nickname or something, right?"

"No." Eyes narrowed, he took a deep breath, turned to me and said, "Justin, I'm an undercover case officer for the Central Intelligence Agency. The CIA."

I shrank away from him. First Scarface, now this. All I needed now was to be kidnapped by some lunatic who thought he was a spy. I grabbed for the door handle to jump out, right into moving traffic.

"*Stop*," he cried. "I'm serious about this. Look, here's my identification." He flipped out an I.D. badge from his jacket pocket.

I hesitated a moment, then took it from him. I gazed hard at it. A thumbprint and mug shot of Bob stared back. Beside them was a silver shield-and-eagle logo over a blue background. Around the picture read the words *Central Intelligence Agency*.

"But . . . but you could make this thing up on any printer," I protested. "And look, it doesn't even say your name on it."

"We leave our names off for security reasons. And no, you won't find those anywhere but CIA."

"Hey, wait a minute. I heard on TV once that the CIA couldn't do spy stuff inside the U.S."

"That was true, at one time. But with the recently expanded Homeland Security powers to combat terrorism, the CIA is allowed to conduct certain covert operations within U.S. boundaries."

"Well, where's your gun? Let me see your gun."

"We rarely carry a gun on field missions, Justin. It only invites trouble. I'm no James Bond."

I sat back, both disappointed and relieved. At least he wasn't going to go nuts and shoot me.

"So you're not a psychiatrist at all, are you?"

He shook his head. "No, that's just my cover story. But you were right the first time. I'm a psychologist. I used to do psych profiles for the intelligence branch. Foreign leaders, terrorists, suspected spies, that type of thing. Until 'The Company' put me in the field as an operative."

"'The Company'?"

"That's what we call CIA in the open, in case someone is eavesdropping."

I stared at Bob for a long moment. Whether he was lying or not, this wasn't the man I thought I was coming to know. And if he *wasn't* who he said he was, I had another psycho on my hands. But if he was telling the truth . . . .

"So what's the CIA want with me? I'm just a New York street kid. I'm not a spy or a terrorist or anything. What did I do?"

He shook his head. "It's not what you did, it's what you might know. And what could happen to you because of it."

"But I don't know anything."

He held up a hand. "Save it, Justin. We're almost there. Everything will be explained by the Director."

"The Director?"

"The Deputy Director for Counterintelligence. You're going to meet him right now."

I gulped and sank lower into the bucket seat.

I half expected Bob to pull into a dark alley and enter a secret hideout, but to my surprise he turned off Washington Memorial Parkway just past a *CIA, Next Right* sign.

I couldn't believe it. Langley, Virginia, CIA headquarters.

We peeled off the main highway, drove up a short road surrounded by heavy woods and came to a ten-foot high chain link, barb wire fence and gate. A Marine peered from the guard booth and checked our license plate before opening the gate. We pulled in. Bob rolled down his window just enough for the guy to inspect his I.D.

The guard bent over and peered suspiciously at me. He said to Bob, "Oh, that's the 'package' we were told to expect. Sign him in here." After Bob did, the guard stood ramrod straight. "You may enter, sir," he announced, waving us on.

We crossed under a surveillance bridge at the entrance that contained who-knows-what kinds of security gizmos. Bob drove through the main car lot. Instead of parking, though, he circled around on a small side road to the back. He turned toward the building and into a driveway. A garage door built right into the building raised automatically, and we pulled up into a tiny parking spot inside. When he stopped, the door closed behind and the whole stall began to sink. The elevator stopped about three floors down. Bob drove into a tiny garage only big enough for eight or ten cars.

We got out. Though the garage looked deserted, the low concrete ceiling seemed to close on me like a trash compactor. We entered a small elevator.

The door closed. He punched an unmarked button. What floor level he picked was anybody's guess. I felt my guts lift as we sank farther underground. Finally the ride stopped. The door slid open.

We entered a typical office corridor like you'd see in any skyscraper in New York, but with no windows. Doors lined the long hallway, along with light blue carpet and freshly painted grey walls. But, except for a couple old aerial photos tacked carelessly to the wall, no flowers or artwork decorated the corridor. The place was dead.

I followed Bob down the hallway, sticking close behind. At the far end of the corridor, two huge oak doors faced us. On them, a brass sign in bold block letters read, *Conference Room*.

Bob turned to me, and for the first time, I realized he was sweating. He straightened my tie and yanked on my jacket sleeves to straighten them. He knocked once, then twice quickly, then once again. I jumped as a lock release buzzed.

"Look sharp," he said, and swung open the doors.

I peeked in. A huge oval table crowded the middle of the small room. Everything, from the furniture to the wall paneling, carried a serious, intimidating look, as if decisions affecting the world were made here. On the far wall hung the same shield-and-eagle CIA emblem I'd seen on Bob's I.D. At the far end of the table sat two men.

Both staring.

At me.

Bob nudged me. I crept in. The man at the head of the table stood and smiled. He raised a hand, palm up, at a sleek office chair near me.

"Have a seat, son," he said. His voice, though soft, had the gruff sound of a commander used to having orders followed.

I sat. Bob took the chair to my left.

The old man began. "I am Allen Cole, Deputy Director of Counterintelligence for the CIA."

"P-pleased to meet you," I squeaked.

"To my left is Mr. Max Hoffman, Deputy Director of Domestic Operations. Mr. Hoffman is Bob's immediate supervisor."

I nodded meekly. Usually I have pretty good eye contact, but Mr. Hoffman's deep green eyes seemed to penetrate my soul. His thin, sandy red hair swooped over his head and a long, stringy Chinese mustache drooped down his chin. When he smiled, he looked like a wizard casting a spell.

Director Cole said, "Son, we brought you here to explain a few things."

"Would you please stop calling me 'son'?"

I shouldn't have let that slip out. Bob raised his brows in alarm.

Cole just smiled. "Okay, uh, Justin. Now, first of all, son, let me say that I'm sorry for the underhanded way we took you from your home. But we had to get you out of the orphanage quickly and quietly. In a way that the enemy wouldn't suspect."

My tie suddenly felt like a noose. Tugging it, I said, "What enemy?"

"This man," Hoffman said, sliding a manila folder across the table to me. Dashed red lines encircled the file, and across one edge read the words, *Top Secret: Operation Rubber Soul.* I hesitated, then glanced at Bob.

He nodded. "Go on, open it."

I did. And spied a photo of the man I most hated and feared in this world.

"Sly Barett," I whispered. "The man who—"

"Killed your father," Cole finished for me.

I slid the file away. "Okay, what's this all about?"

"Mr. Cheney?" Cole prompted.

Bob took a deep breath and began. "After Sly Barett killed your father and escaped from prison, he was never found. We now have reason to believe he's running a drug smuggling operation out of New York."

"But what's this got to do with me?"

"Justin, have you ever heard of the Pharaoh?" Hoffman asked.

I shrugged. "A Pharaoh's one of those ancient Egyptian kings, right?"

"Right," Bob answered. "It's also the code name of the drug kingpin Sly works for. He's also—"

Cole raised his hand. "That's on a need-to-know basis."

"For reasons of national security, you understand," Hoffman explained to me.

I rolled my eyes. "Gee, my Russian contact will be disappointed."

Bob shot me a look of alarm. Hoffman glared at me.

Cole frowned. "We'll ignore that. Just remember son, comments like that get you prosecuted as a spy."

I bit my lip. "Sorry."

"Suffice to say," Hoffman continued, "we don't know who Pharaoh is. That's what were trying to find out."

Bob asked, "Justin, have you ever heard of Operation *Rubber Soul*?"

I shook my head. "Not until now. What is it?"

Bob said, "It's the code name for the drug smuggling operation set up by Sly and Pharaoh."

I crossed my arms. "I still don't see what this has to do with me."

Bob leaned forward and stared into my eyes. "Pharaoh hired Sly Barett to murder your father."

My jaw dropped. *"Hired?"*

Bob nodded. "Pharaoh made a deal with Sly Barett. In exchange for killing your father, Pharaoh smuggled Sly several CIA tools to help him escape prison. While searching Barett's cell, we found a standard CIA lock pick and mini saw disguised as a coat button. Sly killed your father with a single-shot .22 camouflaged as a cigarette."

"But, why?"

Bob raised his palms up. "Apparently, your father stumbled onto the smuggling ring. He then foiled Sly and Pharaoh's operation by stealing the key and access code to the account containing the smuggling profits. And that's why they're after you. They've searched high and low for the key, and now believe your father gave it to you."

Hoffman leaned across the desk toward me, his penetrating green eyes sending shivers up my spine. "Justin. Do you have the key to *Rubber Soul*?"

My lips trembled. "Key? I don't have any key." Then I remembered Scarface, and the note in his wallet about the key. I smirked. I said in triumph, "But I do have your agent's wallet. Remember? That ugly scarred guy you had spying on me at the orphanage yesterday?" I straightened in pride. "Randy picked his wallet and spyPhone clean off him. He never missed it."

The three interrogators exchanged glances.

Bob's eyes grew lined with worry. "Justin, I told you. No one else was at the orphanage with me yesterday. That was one of Pharaoh's men."

CHAPTER 3: SAFE HOUSE

The three men interrogated me for hours, picking my brain for any possible lead. I knew there had to be more to the story about Pharaoh and the smuggling ring and my Dad, but they told me nothing that wasn't "on a need-to-know basis, for reasons of national security," and that kind of crap. Afterward, an artist came in and did a sketch of Scarface, from my description. It was so real it scared me to look at it. Finally, they released me into Bob's custody. Cole ordered me to stay at Bob's house till they caught Pharaoh. My part in their mission was over.

Or so I thought.

By the time we finished the interrogation and drove up to his house, I was zonked out. I awoke as the Vette bounced up the curb into the driveway. I half expected a mansion, but can't say I was too disappointed when I looked up to see a nice Colonial type home, in what I figured was an upper middle class neighborhood. The kind of area where, if me and the orphanage guys went cruising, we'd probably get harassed by the cops.

The garage door opened automatically. We pulled in next to a shiny but older Bronco.

"That yours too?" I asked.

"Yep."

"The Mrs. drive it?"

"Nope. It's not running right now. And I'm divorced."

"Oh. Sorry." It was funny, but I always assumed he was married. I'd never thought to check his ring finger. I wasn't too observant at that time.

"Surprised you're not dirt poor with alimony and all," I said.

He shrugged. "We parted friends. She's well off. A computer analyst."

"Computers, huh?" I asked. "And, I suppose you got one at home, right?"

"Of course."

"We got a couple dinosaur PC's that were donated to the orphanage to play on, but late at night we like to break into Kraut's office and surf on hers. Got any kids?"

"No," he snapped, so sharply that I blinked. He saw my puzzled expression and added, "Sorry. It's just that I . . . ." He held a hand out in invitation. "Why don't I show you around?"

He did. High vaulted ceilings ran through the living and dining rooms in the two-story, three-bedroom house. The giant HD TV blew me away.

"Satellite?" I asked. He nodded.

"No way," I exclaimed. Back at the orphanage all we had was an old junky TV that was stuck on the PBS channel and an ancient DVD player that hadn't worked in years. "Quality programing," Kraut called it. Plus, she'd always add with a frown, it kept us from fighting over what to watch. Think I could recite every *Sesame Street* episode in history. "Woohoo," I shouted, spying the enormous movie library and the huge, crankin' stereo. Two more luxuries I'd never even dreamed of having.

He led me upstairs. The walkway to the bedrooms overlooked the living room and a bay window which faced the front yard. We first came to my room. Bigger than Kraut's office, it even had its own bathroom and shower. Next to the bed a French door and small balcony overlooked the back yard. A grove of maple trees lined the lawn. His room was biggest of course, and it opened off to the middle room which served as a den.

With a hand he beckoned me in. "This is my office when I'm at home," he explained.

I peered inside. Shelves lining the walls surrounded the room with books, too many books. I jumped into the overstuffed black leather swivel chair behind the big oak desk and gave it a spin.

Bob cleared his throat. "Um, there's no need for you to ever come in here while I'm gone. Understand?"

I nodded. "What would I want with a bunch of boring old books, anyway?" I didn't mention that the sweet looking computer on the desk was making me drool.

After the tour, I spent a few minutes alone in my room unpacking my stuff, new and old. I found myself thinking of the guys back home—I mean, the orphanage. Funny how you hate a place so much when you're there, and once you leave you think of it as home.

Looking around my new digs, I said to myself, "Well, *this* is my home now, and I'm not gonna blow it." I leaned my skateboard against the wall by the door, then flopped the duffel onto the bed and pulled my clothes out. Living in a real home again, sleeping in a real bed, in my own private room; it felt great. And best of all, I had a father again, in a way. Dad could never be replaced, of course, but Bob was the next best thing. I decided right then to do my best to stay out of trouble.

Bob knocked lightly on the half-open door.

"Mind if I come in?"

"Not at all, sir."

"Come on, knock off the 'sir' stuff. It's Bob."

"Yes, si—Bob."

He walked in and sat in the desk chair. "Sorry I can't show you around on your first day here, but we've got to catch Pharaoh while the trail's hot. I'll, uh, do something with you this weekend, okay? And we can spend the evenings together this week, after work."

"Ok."

"Sleep in and do what you want tomorrow. Maybe skate around the neighborhood, check it out."

I eyed him skeptically. "You mean, go outside alone?"

He smiled. "Well, you could always stay inside and play Monopoly on the computer."

"Ugh. I hate Monopoly. I'd rather take my chances outside with the Pharaoh."

He laughed at that. "Me too. Look, relax. Pharaoh doesn't know you're here, so you don't have to hide indoors like a trapped rabbit." He shrugged. "Who knows? You might be here for awhile. You need to meet new friends, get used to your new life. One kid, Glen Keller, lives right across the street. A year or two older than you, I believe. Plays varsity football for the high school you'll be attending."

I raised my brows. "High school?"

"Yeah, Plymouth, just down the street. Don't worry, no summer school. You won't start till fall." He crossed his arms. "But we do need to give you a placement test to make sure you can handle your grade. You've done well in school—that is, the few days you've attended."

I flashed an embarrassed grin. "Hmm. Guess I have been slacking in that department."

"We'll spend a few hours brushing up. So . . . what kind of sports do you like?"

"Me?" I stopped unpacking for a moment and thought. "Well, let's see. I've never been one for team sports. I mean, I like watching football and baseball and stuff, but what I really like to do is individual sports."

"Such as?"

"Well, you saw my skateboard. I'm mostly into that, I guess."

"How about martial arts? Do you like Karate?"

"Oh, yeah, that's cool."

"How'd you like to enroll in some classes? Get some self defense training in, just to be on the safe side."

I hesitated. "That'd be neat. But, well, what I really like, is Judo. It's perfect for a small guy like me. Besides, my dad was a fourth degree black belt, and he taught me. I did it a lot when I lived in Japan. But I haven't done it since."

"Really? Well if it's Judo you want, that's what you get. Here's a set of keys to the house and a map I drew of the area. The shopping mall's just a few blocks away." He laid map and keys on the table. Along with a brand new phone. I looked at him.

"Mine?" he nodded. I picked it up and examined it. "A Nostro 650, sweet," I said, playing around with it. "So . . . where does it scan my biometrics to access the CIA database?"

Bob laughed. "Not till you're a level 5 special agent, my friend."

"Say cheese," I said, aiming the phone at his mug.

Bob flashed a silly grin as I snapped. He said, "Wow. For a streetkid, you sure know your way around a cell."

"Are you kidding? Randy and I've lifted hundreds of phones. Fifty bucks minimum on the black market. And they're way easier than wallets and watches."

With a chuckle he said, "I'll keep that in mind. If you have any problems, my numbers are all in there."

"I know," I replied. "Your photo's already loaded on 'em." Within minutes I had it all programmed just the way I like.

His chuckle turned into a yawn. He glanced at his watch. "Well, it's getting late. I've got some last minute work to do, and I go to work pretty early."

He left.

I sat for a long time staring at the door. So much change in so little time. I stripped down, took a long, hot shower, put on my boxers and climbed in bed.

I was dead tired, but I couldn't close my eyes. Visions of Sly Barett and an Egyptian Pharaoh kept popping into my head. I wanted to reach out and strangle them, yet run from them too. I felt so helpless, unable to come up with the tiniest clue that could lead Bob and the CIA to them. If only I knew more about the case. But Cole and Hoffman wouldn't have it. Maybe if I talked to Bob, one on one, he'd let me in on more. I had to try.

I jumped out of bed, threw on my new robe, and crept along the dark corridor to his room. A shaft of light blazed from the crack in his bedroom door. I nudged it open.

"Bob?" I whispered. The guy still intimidated me, so I didn't want to disturb him. I pushed the door farther open.

"H-hello?"

I peered into the room. Nowhere in sight. But I spotted another shaft of light streaming from an opening in the door to his office.

I stepped in. He sat at his desk, his back to me, madly typing away on his computer. On the back of the door behind me, I knocked.

With a yelp, he jumped up and practically out of his skin. Guess I kind of broke his concentration.

"Sorry if I scared you, Bob, but I—"

His face flushed red. "I told you to never enter this room again," he barked.

"Yes, but—"

"No buts, *out!*" He jabbed a finger at the door while his other hand closed a manila folder sitting on the desk by the computer.

Misdirection, that's what magicians call it, when you do something to distract attention with one hand, and with the other steal a card. Or pick a pocket.

Or hide a file.

I glanced at the folder but didn't catch the title written on the front. Just a few random letters.

"Sorry, it can wait." I backed out.

Once in bed with the light out, I lay there thinking about that file. A border of bold red dashes had lined it, like it was important.

"Top Secret," I whispered to the night. That's what it said.

Hot on the trail, I licked my lips and thought of the next line. I hadn't caught any individual letter, but the pattern seemed familiar. The first letter in each word was bigger than the rest. Capitals. O. That was the first capital. The second, R. And the final one . . . S. Operation *Rubber Soul*. The same title as the folder from their headquarters. But with one extra line. I'd only caught a flash of it, yet it seemed most familiar of all. I closed my eyes and tried to remember. Try as I might, my mind came up blank.

No matter. Somewhere in that room, in that Locked Chamber, hid the file. And in that file lay the answers to the mystery of Operation *Rubber Soul*.

I tossed and turned for a couple hours, sweating. No use. I ripped away the covers and crept to the door. I cracked it open.

All the lights were out, including Bob's, so I figured he was sawing logs by now.

The street lamps outside cast a faint glow through the window. I squinted in the dim light, and felt along the wall toward the den. My hand touched the door jamb, then felt along the smooth, varnished oak door to the cool brass knob. I turned it. Locked.

I stood there a moment. My eyes adjusted to the light, and I began to make out silhouettes of things like tables and lamps. And open doors.

Bobs door stood ajar. And, I remembered, his dresser sat right by the entrance. I stared at it, motionless. Patience, Justin, I thought to myself. Too risky.

Well, I've never been one to play it safe, and patience is not one of my virtues. So I edged closer. I paused by the entrance and listened. Bob's soft, rhythmic breathing whispered through the silence. I prayed he was a heavy sleeper. My hands became my eyes as I inched inside the black room and felt for the dresser.

It took five minutes just to move the last two feet as I concentrated on total silence. I felt like a ninja, slinking silently through the night.

My fingers crept up, up to the top of the shelf and along the smooth surface. I heard the soft jingle of keys. Pay dirt! My hand closed around them.

A hand from behind wrenched my wrist into a painful joint lock, while another clamped over my mouth, muffling my scream. The keys dropped from my hands.

Bob's menacing voice whispered in my ear. "You try to steal my money again and the Pharaoh will be the *least* of your problems, hear me?"

I nodded frantically, eyes wide with fear.

"Good. Now, I'm letting you go and you're going back to bed, and *none of this ever happened.*"

I nodded again. He pointed me out and pushed. His door slammed shut.

I grabbed the railing and caught my breath.

Talk about ninja! Man, Bob had snuck up on me and took me out with the skill of a trained samurai assassin.

I trudged back to the room and sank into bed. I lay there a long time, unable to sleep from the adrenaline rush. I mentally kicked myself for screwing up. What a dumb thing to do. Sneak into the bedroom of a CIA agent and try to steal his keys.

But somehow, I thought before drifting off, I had to get into that Locked Chamber and see that file.

* * *

I'm a light sleeper. One small creak of a floorboard and I'm up. That made it tough to sleep in the orphanage, but I learned to live with it.

I awoke to hear Bob shaving. I glanced at the clock. Five a.m. Way too early for me.

I lay silent, listening to his movements as he got ready for work. The moment his Vette roared out of the garage, I pounced out of bed and ran down the hall to the Chamber. I tried the door. Locked. I checked the one in the master bedroom. Ditto.

Slowly, methodically, I searched his dresser drawers and end tables. It was wrong, I knew, but CIA was hiding something from me. Something big. I mean, I wasn't looking for anything private, I just wanted to see that file.

I tried all the usual places. Nothing. But an object buried deep in his dresser drawer caught my attention. A photo. A picture of Bob, smiling, and sitting in a park with some boy about ten years old.

So who was the kid, Bob's son? I wondered. He'd said he didn't have any. Shrugging, I put the picture back.

My search turned up nothing.

I ran and grabbed my Swiss Army lock picks.

I bent to the lock, stuck in the torsion wrench, and went to work with the feeler pick.

With cheap locks I was pretty good, but this thing wouldn't budge. But I kept at it.

The doorbell rang. I jumped, nearly biting my tongue off.

I ran downstairs and answered the door. A guy about my age but a lot bigger, a couple inches taller and muscular, stared back. His blond hair was cropped and his red t-shirt hung out from his jeans. His hands were thrust into the pockets of a blue and yellow Plymouth High letter jacket.

"Justice?" the guy asked.

"That's me. But people call me Justin."

"Hey, Glen Keller from across the street." He held out his hand. I shook it. Strong grip. He shifted from foot to foot and looked around. "Yeah, well I was just sittin' at home, nothin' to do and thought I might come over and introduce myself. You're not busy or anything are you?"

I fought off the urge to say yes. I was dying to search the Locked Chamber, but couldn't. For now. "Nah, I'm not doing anything."

"Oh, good . . . good."

We stood there awkwardly for a long moment, trying to think of something to get the ball rolling.

"So," I said, "you play football?"

"Oh, yeah, for Plymouth. Plymouth High Panthers. You're going there next fall, right?"

I rolled my eyes. "Yeah, I guess so."

"Hey, it's not so bad. Let's see, freshman, right?"

"Ya," I answered.

"I'll be a junior this fall. You play football?"

"Oh, a little bit. But not in school."

"Pop Warner?"

"Nah, just school yard stuff."

"Oh," he said, sounding disappointed.

"I like baseball though."

He lit up. "All right. Wanna throw a bit? Do you have a mitt?" I nodded. "I'll get my ball and mitt and be right back."

I waited for him on Bob's front lawn. As he emerged from his house, I blinked. Behind him followed a slender young girl with wild blonde hair, wearing cutoffs and a guy's muscle shirt. She stopped at the end of the driveway, arms crossed, head tilted, as if to say, "OK, loser, impress me."

Glen trotted up.

I nodded behind him. "And who's that?" I asked.

He glanced behind, then threw a grounder. "Oh, her. That's my sister, Joy."

I suddenly felt all thumbs, fumbling the easy grounder and finally managing to toss it back.

"It's Joy-*ya*," she shot back, in a young but defiant voice. Even from across the street, from beneath that insane tangle of white blonde locks, her pale blue eyes sparkled in the sunlight.

Glen rolled his eyes. "Jo-*yuh*. She thinks she's a Tomboy."

Joya spun and marched inside.

Remembering how good it felt when Bob called me *Justin* instead of *Justice*, I called, "Nice to meet you, Joya!" To Glen I said, "Hottest Tomboy I've ever seen."

His eyes narrowed. "She's only 13."

"But I'm nearly 14," Joya yelled before slamming the door.

Glen beaned a fast one up the middle. I barely caught it before it buried itself in my noggin. "Get that thought out of your head, Justin, or I'll knock it out."

"Ok, I give," I said, laughing and returning the fast ball. "So, how's the school?" I asked.

"Oh, it's okay, I guess. You know, typical high school."

"Yeah. And the girls? Respectfully excluding Joya, of course."

Grinning, he tossed me a high fly. "The finest Virginee has to offer. So, how do you like Mr. Cheney?"

"Bob? Oh, he's okay, I guess."

"He's a psychiatrist, right?"

"Psychologist."

"Whatever."

We played catch all morning, then cruised the mall. By the time we got done, the sun had set, and by the grey twilight we played one last round of catch. He seemed like a pretty good guy, so we made plans to spend the next few days together, playing baseball and stuff. Occasionally, I'd get a glimpse at Joya. Once, she even joined us in a game of pickle. In addition to her wild lion's mane, I found, she had freckles on her nose and cheeks. Amazing, wonderful, light brown freckles.

And, for a girl, she was the fastest runner I'd ever seen.

Bob's Vette wheeled around the corner at the end of the street. I waved to him. Turning into the driveway, he waved back. The garage door opened and he pulled in.

I ran up. "Hi," I said, waving.

He stepped out. "Hey there, sport. Whatcha been up to?"

As his eyes met mine, I froze. His question had sounded innocent, but I felt like he could read my mind. How could I hope to hide anything from a CIA-trained interrogator, and a psychologist at that? I prayed my expression didn't give anything away about the Locked Chamber. I shrugged, and nodded back toward Glen. "Oh, nothing much. Just hanging around with Glen, you know, checking out the neighborhood."

I said goodbye to Glen and followed Bob inside. I stood there on the steps of the living room, shifting from foot to foot, not quite knowing what else to say or do. I wanted to corner him, demand to know what was in that file. But I knew I had to find out myself.

He turned back and looked at me. "Hey, there, make yourself at home. Come on, this *is* your home. Really." He sat down on the couch and patted the seat next to him, inviting me to sit. I did.

We talked small talk for the rest of the evening, avoiding any mention of Sly and Pharaoh and *Rubber Soul.*

I spent the next few days with Glen. Occasionally, I'd get a glimpse at Joya. Once, she even joined us in a game of pickle. In addition to her wild lion's mane, I found, she had freckles on her nose and cheeks. Amazing, wonderful, light brown freckles.

And, for a girl, she was the fastest runner I'd ever seen.

Goofing around with Glen and Joya helped keep my mind off the Locked Chamber. Until something happened that shook me back to reality.

Glen had just got his driver's license and bought an old beat up Mustang, so he and I cruised all around D.C. He played tour guide.

Early Wednesday morning, we left home to go check out the Smithsonian Air and Space Museum. We drove out Dolly Madison Boulevard and took George Washington Memorial Parkway east.

We glided down the tree-lined road. I gazed out the window at the thick forest of maples and oaks, all green and in full spring bloom. The trees whizzed by, posts of an endless picket fence. The low sun flashed between the trunks like a hypnotic strobe light.

Glens voice jolted me back to reality. "Hey, look. CIA, Next Right." He pointed to the sign. He laughed and pulled his shirt collar to his lips as if speaking into a secret microphone hidden in the lining. With a sinister voice he said, "Calling HQ, calling HQ. Secret Agent Shadow reporting in."

I giggled. "Agent Shadow, Agent Shadow, this is HQ, go ahead."

"*Operation Cheeseball* successful. I've got the top secret documents."

"Roger, Agent Shadow. Proceed to the extraction point, over."

"Roger. Be informed the files on double agent Reed, Justice Malcomb, are intact. Request permission to terminate him."

I snickered. "Permission grant—"

I stopped.

The sun popped out from the trees, bathing me in light, then just as quickly disappeared behind the next grove. In that instant, the title of the file flashed into my head:

TOP SECRET
Operation Rubber Soul
Reed, Justice Malcomb

"What's wrong, Justin?"

I swallowed. "Nothin'."

But everything was wrong. That file in the Locked Chamber was all about me.

The CIA sign zoomed by.

Though we spent all day in the museum, my mind never left Bob's office. Once back home, I stood and stared at that Locked Chamber.

I jabbed a finger at the solid door. "Even if I have to use a battering ram, I'm gonna bust in and find out your 'top' secrets. The day is near, my friend."

It was. Two days later, I succeeded.

I was idly watching another lame movie on satellite when Bob got home from work.

Loosening his tie and tossing his briefcase and himself on the couch, he said, "I'm bushed."

"Can I get you something?" I asked.

"Nothing, thanks."

We talked more small talk, like we'd done all week. I had gotten to know him well, I thought, but a thin wall of distrust always seemed to separate us. I knew he was still holding back. Hiding something.

He slapped his hands on his thighs. "Well, off to the showers for me." As he stood, a light went off inside my head.

"Sh-shower, huh?"

"Yep, a long, hot one."

I swallowed, and turned back to the movie as if nothing was happening. I watched, but didn't pay attention. Instead I strained to listen to Bob's movements. He clumped up the stairs, clicked closed the bathroom door and cranked on the radio. The water hissed on.

I sprinted to his room and peeked in. He sang along to the station, his voice filtering through the door in that muffled, echoey tone that only comes from the shower.

I grabbed his key ring and ran next door to the Locked Chamber. I tried each key, found a fit and opened the door. I stopped. Not just yet. No time. I closed it back up, slipped the key off the ring and put the rest back. I flew down the stairs and out the door. On my skateboard, I rocketed down the street. A car screeched to a halt and honked angrily at me. Ignoring him, I skated with all my might to the mall. Popping the skate into my hand as I entered, I ran straight to the key maker's booth. I handed it to him, a geezer who looked older than the planet itself.

"One please," I said breathlessly.

He stared at the key like it was a moon rock. "One?"

"Yes."

After taking it, he paused. "Only one?"

"Yes. Sometime this century, please."

"All right, sonny. Hold your horses." Mumbling to himself, he slowly, methodically searched each and every row of key blanks for the right one. "That's the trouble with kids these days, no patience. Rush, rush, rush. Nooo patience." I tapped my foot as he ground away. After a couple decades he finished.

I raced home and bounded upstairs to his room. I stopped and listened. No running water.

I'm dead, I thought. I returned to my room, leaned against the wooden doorway and breathed deeply, praying he wouldn't notice. Or try to enter his office. I hid the keys under my mattress then took a shower.

Later, during dinner, I made an excuse and slipped upstairs to fit the key back on the ring.

That night I dreamt about the Locked Chamber. It transformed into a giant cave, guarded by a hideous, rotting mummy wearing a Pharaoh's headdress. Fire erupted from his nostrils as he spoke. "Give me the key, Justin. Give me the key or I'll tear you apart, limb by limb!"

I tried to run, but couldn't move.

I awoke with a start, and couldn't fall back asleep. I waited impatiently for Bob to leave for work. As the Vette roared away, I sprinted down the hall. I fumbled for the key, dropped it, and finally got it in the hole. I heard the sweet click of the lock releasing its stubborn grip. I turned the knob.

The Locked Chamber was locked no more.

CHAPTER 4: DEADLY DOUBLE-HEADER

I knew I was alone, but tiptoed in anyway. My heart raced.

Bob's computer gleamed from the desk, inviting. I tried firing it up, but as expected, it was protected by a password. Despite my success hacking into Kraut's computer, I figured my feeble skills were no match for Bob's ultra-modern CIA gizmo. Besides, I wanted that folder with my name on it.

Bob's desk drawers were locked. For the next hour, I picked each one. Beaming with pride and anticipation, I opened each drawer. For all my trouble, however, my treasure proved to be nothing more than a few pens, rubber bands and blank printer paper. The file had to be somewhere else, I figured, like maybe hidden between a couple books.

I set about checking every book. Something struck me as odd. A thin coat of dust covered each book, like they hadn't been touched for awhile. All but one.

Volume II in a series called *Psychiatry A-Z* looked dust free. I pulled the book out and flipped through it. A shred of paper fell out. I opened to the page it had marked. Nothing interesting, just a bibliography about Sigmund Freud. I twitched my lips sideways in disappointment.

I knelt down, picked up the page marker and put it back. I was about to close the book when I noticed something written on the paper. A number, ten digits long. Not a phone number. Scribbled after it read the word "Send." Scratching my head, I put the book away.

I turned to the main book case on the opposite side of the room. Dust coated them as well. The upper shelves, that is.

About halfway through, something strange happened.

I tried to pull a book, but it wouldn't come. An entire row was stuck. The bottom three rows, I learned. I bent close and saw that they weren't books at all, but fake bindings glued to a plastic face.

I pushed and pulled, looking for a way to move the false front. After a half hour of determined searching, I found the trick.

I pulled a book in the left corner of the shelf. It hinged from the bottom, but wouldn't come out. I tried the one on the opposite corner. Same thing. Real, but stuck. I pulled both at once. Bingo.

I heard a faint hum as the false front moved smoothly forward, then up. There, gleaming in metallic mystery, lay my prize. A safe. A huge one, about three feet by three feet. A numbered keypad and two tiny red and green lights occupied the center of its face.

I sat back, both excited and disappointed. If it was locked, no way could I get in. I rubbed my hands and twisted the handle. Yep. Locked.

I sat cross-legged on the carpeted floor, dejected. Key locks I could deal with, but electronic access codes—

Access codes!

I nearly tripped over myself retrieving the book with the paper marker. I knelt in front of the safe.

I reread the scrap of paper. With trembling fingers, I punched each number. After each digit, a high pitched beep squealed in my ears. I punched the button that read *Send*.

The green light blinked three times in concert with the beep, and I heard a faint click as the dead bolts retracted. A green rectangle flashed *Clear*.

Licking my lips, I gripped the handle and twisted. The door swung open. I peered inside, half expecting to find a pirate's treasure chest of gold and jewels. But inside lay a prize far more valuable. Manila folders and a small box sat atop a black briefcase, filling the compartment.

I pulled out the box, peered inside and found a bunch of sneaky espionage stuff like a camera, binoculars, bottle of chloroform, . . . and a "spyPhone" just like Bob's and Scarface's. I was totally tempted to turn it on, but remembered the thumbprint security thing. I set it aside and searched for more goodies. But all that was left buried deep inside Bob's box of dirty tricks was what looked like a bunch of coat buttons and some tiny black pebbles, the kind that you'd get caught in the sole of your tennis shoe. Shrugging, I set the box aside.

I pulled out the files. A chill ran up my spine as I read the title of the first folder.

TOP SECRET
Operation Rubber Soul
Reed, Justice Malcomb

My heart pounded. Suddenly, I realized I was about to become an enemy spy breaking into top secret CIA files. I took a deep breath. No turning back now.

I flipped open the folder and looked at the first document. There, at the top of the page, stood the silver and blue CIA emblem.

The first page described me down to the fillings in my teeth. Age, height, weight, even a photograph. Blurry and grainy, obviously taken from a distance, but you could tell it was me. Riding my skateboard in the courtyard of the orphanage with Randy and Doug.

I leafed through the rest of the file. And learned more about myself than I ever knew. I found photos, news clippings, school test scores, and even a psychological evaluation scribbled in lousy handwriting by some weirdo. And then, I realized with a chuckle, that "weirdo" was probably Bob.

The report said stuff like, "Young Justice Reed, nicknamed Justin, has displayed oppositional and defiant behaviors and has had run-ins with the legal system on numerous occasions. However, there is no evidence of any gang involvement or substance abuse.

"Though understandably rebellious, Justin appears bright enough to resist peer pressure and join a street gang or engage in drug and alcohol consumption. This inner self discipline and conviction is an admirable yet uncommon trait among teen street kids his age."

I snickered at that. But I guess it was true.

One page described my mom, several more my dad, including his Air Force service record in Afghanistan. Randy, Doug, even Glen Keller all had a paragraph or two written about them.

I finished with the dossiers, or whatever you call them, on the people I knew, and leafed through the other folders. Nothing earth-shattering.

Until I came to the folder entitled, *Rubber Soul—Operation Parameters*. Wetting my lips, I opened the file.

I nearly jumped out of my skin when my phone buzzed at my belt, my James Bond ringtone blaring, appropriately, in my ears. I was tempted to let it go to voice mail, but I was afraid it might be Bob. And I wanted to know just where he was at the moment. I took a big breath, then answered.

"Hello?"

"Hey, Justin. It's Glen."

"Hey, bud, how are you?" I asked. But my mind was light years away.

"Listen, there's a baseball game tonight in Baltimore. Orioles and White Sox. I get off work at three. Wanna go?"

"I'd love to. But I'm not sure what Bob's got planned for tonight, so I'll let you know."

"Wanta come over and throw a bit?"

"Nah, not right now. I'm in the middle of—um, a good spy movie."

"Well, come on over whenever you want."

"I'll call you later."

I pushed end before he could reply. I turned back in a trance, every thought focused on the *Rubber Soul* file. I flipped open the folder.

Most of the documents were boring administrative letters sent back and forth between Cole, Hoffman and Bob, and hardly said anything about the actual operation. But toward the bottom, one memo caught my eye.

> Op Rubber Soul—Description.
> Rubber Soul is the code named assigned to an espionage operation directed against the United States government.

"A spy ring," I whispered in surprise. So, there was more to this than drugs. No wonder CIA was involved. I read on.

> Rubber Soul's kingpin appears to be an enemy mole burrowed deep in the CIA network, identity unknown. Code name assigned to this enemy operative, Pharaoh.
> Records show that Pharaoh originally aided CIA in establishing an espionage network during the First Gulf War. Illegally, and against strict operational protocol, he apparently set up a private, concurrent sideline operation, code-named Rubber Soul, to include both drugs and intel. This network appears to have expanded during the

Second Gulf War and beyond. Drugs, intel and money now appear to flow freely between Afghanistan, Iraq and other Middle Eastern sources to New York and D.C. From there, it is speculated, the contraband may continue to other foreign destinations.

Credit for the discovery of Operation Rubber Soul goes to CIA Agent Blue Jay.

I frowned at the last line. My dad had foiled the smuggling operation, not this Agent Blue Jay clown. He told me he'd stumbled onto a smuggling ring when serving in Afghanistan, and promptly reported it to his superiors, but nothing ever came of it. He'd been really bitter about it the rest of his life, saying any drug operation was a direct attack on me. Guess that's why I always shunned the drug scene. That and because they make people act like total morons. So why couldn't they credit Dad for the find instead? I guess in the spy business, the spies got all the glory.

So, Pharaoh wasn't just a druggie, but a spy. A spy hiding in a nest of spies.

One thing I couldn't figure about "Operation *Rubber Soul*," though. Where had CIA come up with such a dorky name for an operation?

For two more hours I read the files, but came up with little more. Finally I quit; my eyes felt bloodshot. I stacked the files exactly the way they had been, and turned to place them back in the safe. I picked up the spyPhone and eyed it.

On a whim, I turned it on. I braced for the lady to come on and bitch me out, saying *"Invalid biometrics scan, access denied. You are an enemy of the State, and hereby terminated."* But to my surprise, the CIA logo popped up full screen, followed by the prompt, *"Initialize."* Not knowing what else to do, I stuck my thumb on it. A bar of light scrolled across the screen and back, and a tiny laser zapped my eyes. I blinked. Onscreen popped the words, *"biometrics and DNA scan complete. Input user name."*

I rapidly typed in, "Justin."

The lady's voice came on again, suddenly sounding all warm and fuzzy. "Welcome, Agent Justin." I decided right then and there that this old broad—I decided to call her Madge—was my new best friend.

But then she said, "Please enter your security pass."

Not knowing what else to do, I typed in my old locker combo. Madge spoke up, suddenly sounding crabby again.

"Invalid entry. Access denied."

I sighed. "Here we go again," I mumbled.

But then she said, "Without a proper security pass, CIA database will be offline and unavailable. However, other basic modes are operational. Would you like to take the tutorial?"

"Holy crap, Madge. Ya!" I exclaimed.

"Very well, Agent Justin. The *Quantum Mark IV*, a substantial upgrade from the *Mark III*, is the new standard-issue, CIA quantum-encrypted cellphone with considerable clandestine enhancements . . ."

I stared at the screen in awe, as Madge walked me through the different features. Along with the database I couldn't get to, it had tons of spy stuff on it. Like one of the devices was a secret bluetooth hidden in the phone, which I promptly stuffed into my ear. The black pebbles in the box turned out to be bugs that the phone would track, and the coat buttons were actually mini spycams. Wild!

After the ten minute tutorial, I just sat there staring at the phone, breathless. Except for a built-in killer particle beam or something, I realized that this magical wonder of technology had everything I needed to hunt down and kill Sly Barett. All I needed was that access code to the CIA database.

"Wait a minute," I exclaimed, bopping my head. "Security pass—Access code. Duh!" I lunged across the room, grabbed the scrap of paper from the book, and typed in the code. *Viola!*

"Access granted, Agent Justin. Welcome to the CIA central database. We have no records on you at this time. Your current clearance level is Twelve beta, minimal clearance. No telephonic or textual communications allowed. To upgrade, please enter Directive Number."

Hoping "minimal clearance" was enough, I typed into their Google-like search window the name, "Sly Barrett." Since there were probably tons of Sly Barett's in the country, I typed in the key phrase, "Attica Prison Break."

Again I sat in awe as Madge narrated a summary of Barett and his life, complete with mug-shots, paper clippings, and a few surveillance photos taken by one spy or another. Then a short video played, an interview with Sly from prison. Shivers blasted up my spine as I listened to his menacing baritone voice. At the end Madge stated sternly, "All current information on Sly Barett requires top clearance level One Alpha."

"Aghh," I cried, nearly pulling out my hair in frustration. I punched the stupid phone off and dumped it back in the box. Setting it aside, I pulled out the black briefcase. As the back of it came away from the edge of the safe, the whole thing clattered to the floor. Heavy.

I pushed outward on the case slide locks with my thumbs. The latches popped with a thud. I raised the lid. And blinked in disbelief. Inside the briefcase were not more files, but instead . . . .

"A pistol," I muttered.

The weapon lay in grey velvet padding. Its shiny black lines and sleek curves reminded me of a black panther.

Menacing, yet sleek and graceful. A cold, beautiful killing machine.

Next to it sat a long, round cylinder about the length of the gun, three clips and a small cardboard box that read, "9mm Cartridges."

I gripped the gun with my hand and felt its weight. I aimed at objects around the room and pretended to shoot.

The cylinder clicked perfectly onto the end of the gun. As I suspected, a silencer. I whipped around and aimed at the door, pretending a couple bad guys were charging me.

Phht! phht! I whistled, imitating the sound of a silencer you always hear in movies.

I looked back in the briefcase. The lid held a black nylon shoulder holster with Velcro straps, which I quickly attached beneath my armpit. The pistol slid perfectly into place, silencer and all. With a shudder, I realized that I was now armed with the perfect weapon to take out Sly once and for all.

Suddenly I felt like a little target practice. Bob would never miss a few rounds, I figured, and I knew I'd need the practice if I really was to hunt down Barett. I opened the box and grabbed a handful of bullets. Recalling my shooting days with Dad, I snapped a full round into a clip, slapped it into the bottom of the grip and slid the pistol in the holster. To hide the weapon, I donned my leather jacket.

I crept downstairs, eyes darting right and left and humming the James Bond theme as I did.

"Agent Justin, superspy of the free world," I said in an announcer's corny voice, "sneaks through the villain's hideout, searching for the beautiful, sexy, bodacious hostage, Suzy Sweetheart."

At the bottom of the steps I quick-drew the gun, spun and pretended to fire. I blew the imaginary smoke away.

"The name's Reed. Justin Reed," I said aloud, mimicking 007's famous line. I shoved the pistol brashly back into the holster.

I stepped into the back yard and glanced around. No one in sight. The garbage can provided me with a tin can target, which I set up at the base of a maple. I stepped back ten paces, flipped off the safety, and aimed. I closed an eye and peered through the sights. Slowly I squeezed. The hammer fell, but nothing happened. I looked at it, bewildered.

"Oh, forgot to cock it," I mumbled. I slid the top of the gun back and heard it chamber a round with a crisp *click-click*. Once again I aimed.

The pistol fired with a *pop*, louder than on TV, and not like the *phht* you always hear. The kick almost knocked the gun out of my hand. I looked through the smoke to see the damage.

"Jeez, some spy I am," I said in dismay. "Missed completely." I searched for a bullet hole in the tree, and found it a whole twelve inches from my target.

My phone rang again. It was a weird number with an i.d. that said, *PiggyMart*, so I figured it had to be Bob calling from some fake CIA phone. I flipped on the safety, holstered the pistol and answered.

"Hello," I answered, breathless.

"Hey, sport, whatcha up to?" came the now-familiar voice of Bob Cheney.

"Oh, um, nothing. Just watching an old rerun." I hoped my voice didn't give anything away. "Uhh . . . are you in the Vette?"

"Yep. Comin' home right now."

"Oh." I froze.

"Ready to go?"

"Go? Go where?"

"Orioles and Sox game. Didn't you see my note on the kitchen table?"

"Where-where are you now?"

"Just turning the corner onto the street. Here goes the garage door."

I heard the hum of the motor. My eyes nearly bugged out of their sockets.

"Meet me downstairs, Justin. Pronto. We've gotta jet if we want to catch the first inning."

I shut off the phone and raced back upstairs, bounding three steps at a time. I sprinted into the Locked Chamber, threw the files and briefcase in the safe and slammed it shut. No time for perfection.

Bob's Vette rumbled into the garage.

I shoved the books back in and the false front slid back into place.

The door clicked open and his footsteps tapped across the floor. I tiptoed out of the chamber and locked the door behind me, leaving no evidence of my presence. I hoped.

I turned to run to my room to hide the gun—he had simply given me no time to unstrap the holster and put it all back. But before I could move, Bob reached the top of the stairs.

"Come on guy, let's jam."

"But, uh, I've got to go to the can." I didn't, but I needed an excuse to get into the room and out of sight.

He started to nod then stopped, cocked his head and looked at me with narrowed eyes. I moved my elbow in to hide the gun.

His face seemed to darken. "No time," he said finally.

"But—"

"You can go when we get there," he barked.

"Yes, sir." When he got cross, I'd already learned, there was no arguing. I followed him to the Vette, and found Glen Keller running across the street to meet us.

"Hey Justin, how's it going?"

"All right, I guess." My head was swimming at the thought of sitting through an entire ball game with a loaded pistol and silencer strapped to my side. "Are you going with us?" I managed to say.

"Yep. Mr. Cheney called and invited me. Thanks, Mr. Cheney."

"Sure. But I told you before, call me Bob."

Glen squeezed his bulky football player frame into the back seat. I dropped into the passenger seat and strapped in, doing my best to cover the pistol with each move. I turned sideways around to talk with Glen. And to hide the weapon.

Bob's car roared to life. He backed out of the driveway and into the street.

I forced myself to think of conversation, but all that came out was a brilliant, "So Glen, whatcha been doin' today?"

"Oh, nothing much," he answered. "Waiting for you to come over."

"Oh, sorry. I got into this great war movie."

"Thought it was a spy movie."

"Oh, yeah. About a spy. And a war. A spy in a war," I finished lamely.

As I looked back and talked, I noticed through the rear window a pair of auto headlights come on. The car, parked on the street a few houses down, pulled into our lane but kept back a ways.

"You boys ready for a double-header?" Bob asked.

"Oh, it is?" Glen asked. Bob nodded. "In that case, mind if I use your phone to let my mom know? She borrowed my cell."

Bob pointed to his phone, sitting in its cradle on the t-bar. "Sure."

I slid it out and handed it to him. "Just push the Memory 3 icon on the touch screen. Bob let me program your cell into it."

Glen smiled. "Really? Cool, thanks."

After he was done, he tried to hang it up, but had trouble.

I took the phone from him. "Here, it's a bit tricky. You have to push the Off button or it won't hang up. Then it slides into the charger cradle like this." As I hung up the phone, my jacket flashed open. I pinned my arm to my side and glanced at Bob.

He just watched the road, apparently clueless. He said, "Say, Justin, you got a friend who lives in Baltimore, don't you?"

"Yeah, Carlos Martinez. He used to be in the Air Force with my dad out in Afghanistan," I answered absentmindedly. I couldn't believe Bob had missed the gun. That was a close one.

We chatted all the way to the stadium. The other car kept with us right around Capital Beltway and up I-95. They even turned off at the same exit in Baltimore. So the neighbors were baseball fans, too, I figured.

The Orioles stadium wasn't too crowded yet, so we got to park up close. We shuffled through the turnstiles. I heard the crack of a bat followed by cheers. I ran forward to an entrance to catch the action.

Bob called after me, "Hey there. Thought you had to go real bad."

"Oh, yeah." I stomped off to a bathroom out in the corner of the stadium behind the field. Bob and Glen waited at the entrance.

As I entered, Bob said behind me, "Glen, why don't you go find our seats?"

The bathroom was empty, so I walked to the nearest urinal and stood there for a minute, acting the part in case Bob came in. He did. I pretended to zip up then flushed the stall.

He stood by another urinal. "I'll be out in a minute."

"Okay." I turned to leave.

Two men wearing ski masks and overcoats entered and rushed over to us. The first man grabbed my arm.

"Hey, what the—" I froze mid-sentence. A jolt of fear raced through me as I spotted the jagged line running down his neck. Scarface!

Bob wheeled around to defend us, but Scarface whipped out a pistol from beneath his coat and held it to the side of my head. Attached to his gun was the long barrel of a silencer.

"Don't move, Cheney," Scarface growled. "We just want the boy. Frisk him, Marco."

The other man searched Bob. Hands raised, Bob said, "Leave him alone. He knows nothing."

"Shut up, Cheney. Pharaoh thinks otherwise."

"He's clean, boss," Marco said.

"Good. Tie him up."

Scarface yanked me, and we backed slowly toward the door.

Marco slapped a piece of duct tape around Bob's mouth then wrapped his wrists with the silver adhesive.

Scarface bumped against the door jamb and, in the distraction, relaxed his grip. I wrenched free and with all my might elbowed his stomach. He yelped and doubled over. I jumped away, tripped and fell backward.

Bob, hands tied, sprang into action. He kicked Marco in the nose, sending the kidnapper to the ground, then stomped his ribs. Bob raced over and kicked Scarface's gun from his hand. The pistol clattered against the wall. Bob continued into a spin kick that whizzed by Scarface's nose. The two pounced on each other. Marco jumped in. Bob, hands bound, had no chance. Marco yanked Bob away while Scarface lunged for his pistol, turned and aimed at Bob.

With trembling hand I slid the gun from beneath my shirt and brought it up. I cocked it with a *click-click*.

The kidnappers whirled around in surprise.

Scarface brought his gun around to aim at me. Water filled my eyes and everything turned blurry. Remembering my poor practice shot at Bob's, I feared that I might hit him instead. I aimed above them.

I closed my eyes and fired.

Chunks of brick wall exploded beside them. Scarface screamed. He dropped the gun and held his eyes. Blood began to oozed between his fingers and dripped to the floor.

Marco lunged for the gun, but Bob kicked it away. Marco grabbed Bob and shoved him against the wall, his head striking the brick and stunning him momentarily. Marco grabbed Scarface and dragged him out the door.

I froze, horrified. I had nearly shot another human being.

Bob ripped the gag from his mouth and bounded toward me like a charging rhino.

"Untie me," he demanded.

I pulled the duct tape away from his wrists.

He yanked the gun from my hand, popped out the clip and flipped on the safety. He opened my jacket and shoved the pistol into its holster. With a handkerchief, he picked up Scarface's pistol and slid it into his pocket.

"Th-that was Scarface," I stammered, my voice barely audible.

"Shut up."

Bob bent close and drilled me with a look of fury. Veins bulged from his neck. "This never happened. Let's go."

He stormed past me. I stared, transfixed, at the blood splattered on the floor. Bob grabbed my collar and yanked.

"I said, Go." He hauled me like a rag doll out the door.

Bob barricaded the bathroom door with a "Closed for Cleaning" sawhorse nearby. Punching his spyPhone, he called headquarters. "Shrink here," he announced. "Code 16. Cleanup and CSI crew, this GPS location, ballpark East Entrance men's room. Priority one." He was talking gibberish, but I could figure out what it meant.

As we walked to our seats, the sniffles began. A tear ran down my cheek. With my shirt sleeve I wiped it away.

"Knock that off or our guest will know something's wrong." Nodding, I did my best to suck it in.

We watched the game, pretending like nothing had happened.

Glen noticed my flushed look and snively nose though. He patted me on the back.

"What's the matter, Justin?" he asked.

I opened my mouth to answer, but Bob beat me to it.

"Nothing." The way Bob said it made Glen shut up.

I kept listening for ambulances and cop cars, but they never came. I kept glancing over my shoulder, half expecting a detective to grab me and say, "You're under arrest for attempted murder." But it never happened.

My head swam. Inning blurred into inning, Glen quoting baseball stats and me mumbling lame replies. Between games, we ate at the snack bar. My stomach churned, and I burned with fever. All I wanted was a soda for my dry mouth. But Bob grabbed me and whispered in my ear, "Eat your food like nothing's wrong. Hear me?"

I nodded. I forced a hot dog and chips down, then concentrated on keeping them there.

We took our seats. Sweat trickled down my cheeks. The liquids in my stomach bubbled and sloshed like waves in a jacuzzi.

"Bob, I have to go to the—"

"Stay here."

But I couldn't hold it in. I grabbed an empty popcorn bag and lost my cookies. Or, should I say, my chips.

Bob looked at me and sighed. "I'm sorry, Glen. Looks like Justin got a bad piece of food tonight. We'd better go."

"Hey, no problem." Glen patted me on the back. "Justin, buddy, you okay?" I looked up and nodded. My face must have been as white as the Orioles' uniforms.

When we left, I glanced at the bathroom doorway. The sawhorse that read Closed still blocked the entrance, but men in janitor jumpsuits now darted about the area as if cleaning. But I knew they were really CIA agents, investigating—and erasing—the incident.

We drove home in silence. After an eternity, we pulled into the garage.

As Glen emerged from the car, he forced a nervous laugh. I could tell he sensed the tension between us.

"Well, great game guys," he said. "Thanks for the ticket, Mr. Che-uh, Bob. Well, I oughta get going. Hope you feel better Justin." He bolted home.

Once inside, Bob turned on me. He held out a palm. "Give it to me."

I obeyed, unable to look up past his shoes, like a puppy caught stealing a scrap from the table.

"Knew I should have confiscated the thing when I got home," he mumbled half to himself, grabbing the weapon from my hand. "But I wanted to teach you a lesson."

"You *knew*?" I asked in surprise. His glare was his answer. I withered. "I'm sorry."

"Quiet. Get straight to bed. You've got a long day tomorrow. You're going with me to headquarters."

CHAPTER 5: A SPY IS BORN

"Get up."

I forced my eyes open. Bob's shadow loomed over me.

"Take a shower and get dressed. Suit and tie. We leave at oh-six hundred. Not one second later." He slammed the door.

Boy, was I cooked. I trudged to the bathroom and stared at myself in the mirror. I said to my reflection, "Way to screw up, Justin. Now I'll never get my hands on Sly Barett."

Back to the orphanage for me, I was sure—after getting a thorough reaming from Bob and his superiors. Then on to the wrath of Kraut.

Once downstairs, Bob knotted my necktie once again, his mouth twitching sideways in annoyance. Again I didn't feel like food, but he forced me to eat the eggs he'd made. We said nothing.

He practically dragged me by my ear out to the car. He pulled out with a screech, and we flew down the road. On the way there, he briefed me. He talked sideways to me as he concentrated on the road.

"After last night's attempted kidnapping, we've got to refigure our game plan. Especially now that you know so much. You *did* read the files, didn't you?"

I held up the duplicate key I had made.

"I see. You realize that's espionage, don't you?"

"But I only wanted to help, and Cole and Hoffman wouldn't—"

"Irrelevant. Actually, Cole thought you might get around to that. But we had no idea it would be so soon." He shook his head. "I *knew* I should've confiscated the gun. But I wanted to make you sweat it out. Teach you a lesson."

I turned to him. "How'd you know I had the gun?"

With a glance to me, he said, "When I got home from work, I inspected you. Did what we call a *mental frisk*, and spotted the weapon under your jacket. I didn't expect you to have anything, of course, but it's second nature for a field agent to inspect everyone."

"Those men had followed us—"

"Save it for the meeting."

I shut my mouth. We said little more. Once inside CIA, I trotted to keep up with Bob as he marched to the conference room.

Cole and Hoffman sat quietly at the table. Both staring. At me.

Cole said, "Have a seat, son. I want you to watch a video."

I sat. The lights dimmed, and the CIA emblem on the wall faded to a blank white screen. An image flickered.

The image of the Locked Chamber. I could see the entire room; a video camera must have been hidden in the far back corner of the office. Time and date flashed in the lower right hand corner of the picture.

I watched in disbelief as a speeded up, time lapsed image of myself appeared in the doorway. I flew through the room, inspecting each book, ending with the safe and its secret contents. It was almost comical. But I wasn't laughing.

The lights came up.

"How did you get that?" I asked.

Bob said, "Motion-activated security camera. The image is relayed here and recorded on the central database."

Cole said, "As you can see, we know everything."

My stomach felt like a slug of molten lead. I trembled. "Wha-what now? Prison?"

"Hmph," Bob snorted, "that would probably be the safest place for you."

My eyes widened. "You don't really mean—"

Cole raised a hand. "Of course not, son. As I said, We know everything."

Hoffman added, "And so, apparently, does Pharaoh."

"What?" I asked. "How could he possibly know?"

The three spies exchanged glances.

Cole shook his head. "We've been discussing that very question all night. He must have known all along."

Bob rubbed his chin. "He must be much higher up the CIA than we first thought."

Hoffman nodded. "Either that, or he's got one helluva spy network."

Cole turned to me. "Or both. Whatever the case, he's been patiently waiting to make his move on you. But when he saw you break into the files he must have feared you'd find something that would jog your memory of the case. So he panicked, and tried to kidnap you last night."

"Lucky for us he didn't think you'd use that pistol," said Hoffman.

Cole said, "Good reaction, son. We're not happy about what you did in Bob's office, but in this business, reactions like that can save a man in the field."

"Or a kid," Bob added. "Thanks, Justin. You saved me too."

I lowered my eyes and forced a smile.

Bob shook his finger at me. "Just don't do anything stupid like that again, hear me?"

"Yes, sir."

Cole sighed. "So now the question is, what to do with you."

"Witness protection program," Bob said flatly.

Cole shook his head. "Useless, under the circumstances. Pharaoh's anticipated our every move. He'd no doubt be ready for that as well."

"Then we've got to keep Justin under constant surveillance," Bob replied. "There's no other way. Not until we catch Pharaoh."

Hoffman held up his palms. "That could take years. We're farther from catching him than ever."

"And we can't keep the boy locked up forever," Cole added.

Unable to come up with a solution, the three spies fell silent.

A light went off in my head. Here was my chance to catch Pharaoh *and* Sly. I looked up and spoke.

"He panicked once. He could panic again."

All eyes turned to me.

"Go on," Cole prompted.

I licked my lips and leaned forward. "Okay, look. Pharaoh thinks I know stuff, right? And he thinks I have the key to his *Rubber Soul* account. So why don't we give him what he wants? Let him capture me, and you can—"

"No way," the three chorused.

Bob added, "We've got to protect you."

"The only way to protect me now is to catch him," I countered.

"Justin, he's a killer. He'll—"

I pounded my fist on the table. "I know! He killed my dad, remember?"

The three men said nothing, just stared.

I sighed, then lowered my voice. "Look, send me back to the orphanage. Then you keep watch. And when Pharaoh grabs me again, you nab him."

Bob shook his head and sat back. "Not a chance, Justin."

"I'm the best chance you've got."

Stroking his stringy mustache as if lost in thought, Hoffman said, "Perhaps the boy has an idea."

Bob's mouth dropped open. "*What?*"

"Hmm," Cole said in reply, apparently matching Hoffman's thought. "Sometimes the safest place for a deer to hide is in the hunter's camp."

Bob stood and slammed his palms on the table. He leaned forward. "This is absurd. You'd be placing a civilian, a boy no less, in *extreme* jeopardy." He waved a hand. "Besides, Pharaoh would know it's a set-up. He knows we wouldn't just abandon Justin back at his orphanage."

Hoffman's eyes lit up. "So we spread word that we think we've caught the Pharaoh. Then we put Justin back in the orphanage. But we have *two* men watching him. The first will be a plant, a fake body guard. We wire Justin with a bug which the second guard, the real guard, tracks. Pharaoh distracts the fake guard and tries to nab Justin." He waved his hand and clenched his fist triumphantly in the air. "But instead, we bag Pharaoh."

Bob folded his arms. "Oh yeah, Max? And what if we miss?"

"That's why we wire Justin," Cole said, catching on. "Backup plan. The second man tracks Justin to Pharaoh's hideout, cases the joint, and calls in the cavalry when the time is right." Again Hoffman flashed that wizard's grin. "Foolproof."

Bob hunched forward. "Why do I shudder whenever I hear that word, foolproof?" Bob sat back and once again crossed his arms. "I don't buy it, gentlemen. Way too risky. We can't protect the boy from a ghost."

"Safety measures would be taken," Cole said softly.

Bob stared at the other two for a long moment. His nostrils flared. "You're my superior officers; I have no say in this. But if you go through with this, you do so under my vigorous protest."

"Noted," said Cole.

Bob jabbed a finger at Cole. "If we're not there to help him at the crucial moment, he'll have to think on his feet, and fend for himself. He needs full CIA training if we expect him to survive."

I perked up at that.

Cole's brows knotted in thought. "We'd need to hide him for awhile anyway, until we're ready. And if we abandoned Justin too soon after last night's attempt, Pharaoh would smell a rat." He looked up. "Actually, a training course as you describe is already in place for just such a contingency. Its code-named Operation *Lenin Star*."

Here we go again with goofy code names, I thought. *Lenin Star* sounded like some spy operation in Russia, not a training camp. Just like Operation *Rubber Soul*. Still couldn't figure that one out. I'd wracked my brain for days to find a clue to that name. Dad had owned an old Beatles album named *Rubber Soul*, I remembered. But all I knew about the Beatles were their names, John Lennon, Ringo Starr, Paul McCartney, and George Harrison.

Cole continued. "Bob, we'll brief you on *Lenin Star*, and you can run the training op personally for Justin. In two months' time, if Pharaoh isn't apprehended, we'll go with the plan." He turned to me. "Son, it's your call. We can't force you to do this. Think long and hard before you answer."

Hoffman lifted a finger. "Be warned, Justin. If you say yes, then from here on out, nothing will be easy. And as Bob mentioned, there could be some risk involved. But if our plan works, we'll have Pharaoh. *And* your father's killer."

I stared at the table. Sweat trickled down my forehead. Me, trained by the CIA! Any kid would jump at the chance. And if anyone could track down Pharaoh and Sly, a CIA agent could. But I knew this schoolyard fantasy could get me killed.

I had no choice. I took a deep breath.

"I'll do it."

Cole narrowed his eyes. "You realize there's no turning back—"

"I said I'll do it."

Cole sat back, relieved. He turned to Hoffman. "You want to coordinate this, Max?"

Hoffman took the cue. "All right, Justin, it's off to summer camp with Bob. But this will be no walk in the woods like you're used to." I had never gone to summer camp, but I caught his drift. "This will be a special camp, with you as the only member. You'll devote the next eight weeks of your life to training. You will eat, sleep and breathe training. You will study the knowledge and practice many of the skills necessary for a field intelligence operative. And Bob will be there to guide you through it all."

I nodded. "Just like Fagin and Oliver."

Cole looked puzzled. "I beg your pardon?"

"You know, Charles Dickens. *Oliver Twist*, where the robber Fagin and the Artful Dodger taught Oliver how to be a thief."

Cole folded his arms, sat back and grinned. "Exactly. Yes, just like in *Oliver*."

Hoffman said, "You will be taught highly specialized skills such as covert surveillance, intelligence gathering, unobserved target area penetration, self defense, and enemy disposal techniques."

I had to admit, the guy had lots of fancy names for spying, stealing, fighting and killing.

"Where do I train? Here?"

Cole laughed lightly, as if I was a dunce. Guess I was.

"No, son. You've got to be kept absolutely secret. We can't even use The Farm, CIA's standard training facility. You'll be sent to what we call a "safe house." The Pharaoh will think we're merely hiding you. He'll expect that." Cole turned to Bob. "Cheney, there is to be no paperwork on this, understand?"

Bob hesitated before grumbling, "Yes, sir."

Cole looked to Hoffman, "Max, whip up some files explaining that Justin knows nothing—absolutely nothing— and is being held in an undisclosed location pending further breakthroughs in the investigation. Send them through the standard channels. If Pharaoh intercepts it, and I expect he will, that should appease him for the moment."

One question left. "When do I start?"

The three men traded a look. Cole turned to me, eyes narrowed. "Faster than you can say, '*Oliver Twist*'."

* * *

I was sent to another "safe house" nearby, sort of a small hotel for spies, I figured. The place had no windows and was surrounded by Marine guards, some even hidden in the woods. For two days, I lounged around, bored, not knowing what to do with myself. At least the TV kept me company. And then, Bob walked in holding a piece of paper.

He laid it on the desk. I peeked over his shoulder to read it, but it looked like gibberish. Random letters and numbers, like a monkey had typed on a computer then hit Print. Bob slowly scribbled out the translation of each character, using what he called a one-time decipher pad—translate only one message, then the key's no good so you burn it.

Fm King Cole
To Fagin/Dodger

I smirked. "Fagin and Dodger, hmm?"

Bob nodded. "Our code names. I'm Fagin, you're the Artful Dodger. Cole seemed to take to your analogy of Dickens. But he thought you were more the roguish Dodger type than the angelic Oliver."

I rolled my eyes. "*Greeat*," I mumbled with a chuckle.

He deciphered the rest. I read.

Op Lenin Star activated.
Report immediately to Safehouse Delta-Q for training.

My spy career had begun.

*   *   *

I told everyone that I was off to live at Bob's psych clinic full-time for his "experiment." I even had to send fake post cards to Glen, and Randy and Doug at the orphanage. CIA happily provided false postage marks.

Bob stayed with me most of the time and directed the training.

We woke up every morning at 5 a.m., a torture that I learned to enjoy once I got into the habit. Before breakfast, I jogged. Bob ran with me. And blew me away. I could only go a couple miles the first week, but I gradually worked up to six before breakfast.

Half the day, I attended school. But instead of boring history or algebra, I studied wild subjects like weapons, electronic bugs and wiretaps.

Experts in each field taught me the trades. In fact, so many instructors taught me, I could hardly remember their names—another skill I was learning, observation and memory improvement. Each one easily remembered my name though.

It seemed strange that, if this was all supposed to be so secret, why did they give me so many teachers? And why did they call me by my real name, instead of my code name, Dodger?

In surveillance class, I learned how to use lots of secret gadgets, including the "spyPhone" I'd seen in Bob's safe. It did way more than even the tutorial had said, too, including tracking the user. Bob said they would use it to follow me during the mission. The coat button spycam had a range of a couple city blocks, or a mile if used simply as a listening bug. The black pebble tracked up to five miles, though you couldn't hear conversations with it.

I learned the art of the *mental frisk*, like Bob had done to me. You search for weapons on a guy by spotting bumps in his clothing or watching the way he walked, favoring a certain location on his body.

In escape class, I gleefully got to perfect my lock-picking techniques. I learned to drive, too. And not in a boring minivan or a simulator like high schools have, but a totally mean-looking Camaro Z-28. Old, beat up and painted dark green with patches of primer gray, it didn't look like much. But the V-8 under the hood packed a wallop. I nicknamed it *Shadow*, in honor of Glen's fake secret agent.

I blasted around the obstacle courses at top speed. I learned lots of stunts, like high speed turns, brodies and donuts, and how to weave through heavy traffic.

Next came weapons class. Everything there was to know about guns and knives, and the secret weapons used by agents, I learned. For target practice, I mostly shot a Colt Mustang PocketLite .380. The tiny pistol fit easily into my palm. I got a kick out of rapid-firing all seven rounds, popping out the clip (the proper term was *magazines*, I'd learned), slapping in a new one, and squeezing off six more. Sometimes I even shot with a silencer attached.

I loved the thrill and power of it all—the flash of flame, the kick of recoil, the loud report. The satisfaction I felt blasting apart the paper targets I imagined to be Sly Barett or Pharaoh. But another side of me dreaded the danger of this weapon, the seductive, double-edged sword that it was. The feeling worsened during practical training, where I had to think on my feet and to escape, avoid capture, or even "dispose" of the enemy.

But enemy or not, Sly and Pharaoh were real, living people. Could I really feel proud to shoot, maybe even kill, another human being? At the ballpark I couldn't bring myself to shoot Scarface, even though he was ready to shoot me. And each time during practice that I fired a blank or stabbed with a rubber knife, a tiny voice whispered in the back of my mind, *Don't do it, Justin. Don't become one of them.*

Revenge and guilt, guilt and revenge, bounced back and forth in my head like tennis balls at Wimbledon.

In the late afternoon came homework. After dinner they gave me one hour of free time, which I usually spent fast asleep. The last hours before bed brought more physical training, including self defense. Practice focused on open-hand fighting, since I'd most likely be unarmed.

As promised, I got back into Judo. And Kung Fu and Brazilian Ju Jitsu and Thai Boxing and Israeli Krav Maga . . . Bob taught me the best techniques from the best martial arts, plus boxing and plain old, dirty street fighting.

During self defense class, I grew closer to Bob than ever before. He turned out to be a black belt in Judo, just like Dad had been, so practicing with Bob brought back good memories.

But one time I got too close to him.

Bob had been teaching me a foot sweep, *de ashi harai*, and when I tried it on him, I caught his foot just right and he dropped like he'd slipped on a banana peel.

I laughed in triumph. "Ha, I got you!"

He laughed, then gave a strange reply. "Yeah, you got me, Eddie." His smile faded, and his whole face darkened. "I mean, Justin."

We stared at each other for a long moment. I recalled the picture I found in his desk drawer, the one with him and the boy. I narrowed my eyes.

"Who's Eddie?"

He frowned, cleared his throat and stood. "Forget it. Hit the showers." I didn't budge, just stared at him. "Now."

I turned away, sighing in frustration. My orphanage days had taught me to pick the toughest of locks, but I couldn't pick the one that guarded Bob's heart.

And who was this Eddie, anyway? As I stripped and showered, my mind explored the possibilities. Bob still insisted he had no kids. But he'd been married, and now was divorced. Yes, divorced. That was it.

I nodded confidently and said to myself, "So, his Ex has custody of his son, whose name is Eddie, and he never gets to see him."

The next day, Bob's boss Max Hoffman showed up for a surprise inspection. He gave me the willies, smiling his wizard's smile as I demonstrated my new skills. But he complimented me at the end by saying, "You would have made your father proud." That seemed strange. There was no way he could have ever known my dad. Guess it was just a saying that he used.

Later, we tried some dry runs with the double body guard plan. One day a week I stayed at Bob's house. When I played ball with Glen, he never spotted our tails, though sometimes I did. When we hung out at the mall, I chose random shoppers and practiced tailing them as well. Glen never even caught on that I was doing it. Of course, I always made sure my surveillance target was a cute girl.

Late in the summer, I graduated from the *Lenin Star* course. I passed Spy 101 at the top of my class. Of course, I was the only one *in* my class.

Back at CIA headquarters, Cole and Hoffman interviewed me.

Hoffman sat to the side while I stood facing Cole across his massive desk. He leaned back in his plush chair, his old blue eyes squinting at my file through a pair of bifocals. I recalled my times in Kraut's office, sweating on the carpet while she read my files and decided what delightfully cruel punishment to dish out.

Cole closed the folder and looked up.

"Impressive. Says here your progress has been remarkable. Exceeded even our expectations. Bob says you learn things quickly, and despite your small size fight with a spirit and drive unmatched."

I recited a Dickens line. "Somewhat diminutive in stature, but nature or inheritance had implanted in him a good sturdy spirit."

Cole smiled. "Let me guess—*Oliver Twist* again, right?" I nodded. Hoffman grinned. Cole took off his specs and stared up at me. "We haven't found a trace of the Pharaoh. Since you went underground, so did he. My guess is, since we turned up the heat, he's cut his losses and run. He'll expect that of us, and will think it completely logical that we would send you back to the orphanage." He leaned across his desk. "The time has come for your mission."

I swallowed. "I'm ready."

Cole tapped his specs against his palm. He stared at the lenses, his eyes avoiding mine. Finally he looked up.

"Son, this is hard for me to say. I want you to know that I would never intentionally subject you to any known danger. But until Pharaoh is caught, your life will always be in jeopardy. I find myself at a loss as to any other way to—"

I held up a hand. "You don't have to explain, Mr. Cole. I've got my own reasons for doing this."

"I understand your motivation, son. Nevertheless, Justin, your country is grateful for your service."

The line sounded phony, but I didn't care. "Sure. Whatever."

Hoffman said, "Just remember: none of this ever happened."

* * *

Since CIA had given me a fake New York driver's license, on our trip home from Langley, Bob let me drive the Vette.

Once inside the house, he opened the Locked Chamber and fired up the computer.

"There are some last-minute briefs you need to read before we send you to the orphanage," he said as he patched us into CIA's intranet on a quantum-encrypted modem, which was practically untappable. He called up the notes and I sat down to study. After an hour, I sat back and rubbed my bloodshot eyes.

"How about a Coke?" Bob asked.

"That would be great," I said through parched lips.

He walked toward the door, then lingered a moment. "Justin, I still think this plan stinks. Just remember, no matter what Cole says, you can back out any time."

I looked him straight in the eyes. "I'm going to find my father's killer, and no ghost, goblin or Pharaoh is going to stand in my way."

He stared at me a long moment, then gave a slight nod.

"I'll be right back." He left.

This was the moment I'd waited months for. Here I sat, alone, with the CIA network, completely unrestricted, at my fingertips. Now I could search for the data I needed to find Sly on my own.

I jumped up and switched off the power to the video camera. From CIA training, I knew right where to look. Into the computer I typed, "Access Link: FBI National Crime Information Computer (NCIC) Data Bank; Fugitive List; Barett, Sylvester."

His file popped up. I skimmed through it.

I heard Bob close the fridge door. No time for details. I punched a button, and the laser printer silently zapped me a copy. I stuffed the page in my pocket, erased the internet history, then called back up the training file. Just before Bob rounded the corner into the room, I flipped on the video camera then pretended to be gazing out the window.

"Gets tiring, doesn't it?" he said.

Biting my lip, I turned to him. "Bob, remember back when I broke in here and found the CIA files?"

"How could I forget? I don't think I could've done as good a job."

"Thanks. But there was something else I found. A photograph. Of a kid. That's Eddie, isn't it? And Eddie's your son, isn't he?"

His lips tightened. That same darkened expression returned to him. He opened his mouth, closed it, then his brows drooped. He looked at the floor. After a moment, ever so slightly, he nodded.

"Living with his mom, right?"

Without raising his head, he slowly looked up at me. Never before had I seen his eyes so lifeless.

"He died of a drug overdose when he was twelve."

My mouth dropped open. The wind escaped from my pipes like someone had punched me in the gut. "I'm sorry. I had no idea."

He shrugged. "That's the main reason Janice and I split up. We kept blaming ourselves. And each other, I guess."

I saw Bob in a new light. Not just as a kind man, but as one who had experienced—and understood—what I went through with Dad.

He spread out his hands. Tears welled up in his eyes. "I should have told you, Justin. But I miss him so much, and now you're here and it's like it was before, and . . . ." His voice trailed off.

I felt the same way. I missed Dad, but Bob was fast becoming a second father to me. "Is that what you want? Another son?"

He swallowed, and answered slowly. "This . . . this is the wrong time to discuss it, Justin. There's still things I . . . have to work through first. Look, you're about to leave, go back to the orphanage. When all this is over, maybe we can talk about it, okay?"

I forced back a tear and buried my emotions. That seemed to be the adult way to deal with problems, I was learning.

"Okay," I whispered.

He ruffled my hair and smiled. "How about catching dinner and a flick with Glen and Joya?"

We did. But I couldn't concentrate on the movie, let alone Glen's lovely, wild sister sitting next to me.

It seemed so bizarre to scheme plans of international espionage one minute, then go out on the town with friends the next. And thoughts kept swimming through my head. Tomorrow, I knew, I would leave Bob for good. Abandoned again, just another orphan. But something far worse than loneliness awaited me on the mean streets of New York.

Pharaoh.

CHAPTER 6: THE DODGER AS BAIT

Not until I crawled into bed that night did I get a chance to look at the rap sheet I'd printed on Sly.

Pulling the crumpled paper from my trouser pocket, I stripped to my boxers and flipped off the bedroom light. I got under the covers and switched on the night lamp. The shaft of light pierced the darkness like an interrogator's beam. I read.

NCIC Data File
Subj: Sylvester "Sly" Barett
Known Aliases: Saul Barrister, Bart Slymann
History: Former CIA agent, Mideast theatre.

"Holy—"

I sat bolt upright. Sly, an agent? CIA had lots of shady contacts, I knew. But a convicted murderer? I read on.

Criminal History:
Six separate felony charges, including Distribution of Narcotics; Inciting Prostitution; Assault. All charges dropped, reasons unkn. Armed Robbery, Assault, Second Degree Murder; sentenced to 40 years in Sing Sing max. sec. prison. Xferred to Attica max. security prison, reasons unkn.

So, after his run with CIA, Barett had gone on a crime spree. But Pharaoh had obviously pulled strings to get all Sly's charges dropped, up to the last one, a biggy, armed robbery and murder. No one short of a governor could get him off that one. I read the rest.

> Escaped Attica prison, killing guard Malcomb Reed in the process; current whereabouts unkn. Suspect possible location New York, NY; poss. affil. w/The Bones, a New York street gang suspected in prostitution/ drug smuggling ring. FBI currently investigating.
>
> ATTN: SUBJ CONSIDERED ARMED AND EXTREMELY DANGEROUS.

As I read the last few lines about the prison break and Dad's murder, a tear dribbled down my cheek. With the bed sheet I wiped my snively nose.

As always, sorrow gave way to anger. My fingers tightened around the page, crumpling it like a crisp leaf.

I shook the fog from my head. There had to be a clue in there somewhere. I reread the last few sentences, and found it. The Bones gang, in New York. So Sly had returned to his home town.

I pulled from my wallet an old news clipping of the prison break. In the middle of the article, a photo of Dad smiled back. From another scowled a mug shot of Sly. I reread the yellowed article and found it. Barett's old address.

Sly couldn't go near his old house; FBI would have it cased. But he'd be in the area.

And so would I.

I knew the Bones. Bad group of boys. Another useless street gang, good for nothing but ruining the lives of its members and their victims. One of the biggest groups of thugs, too. Even Randy's tough gang friends were scared of them.

Yawning, I rubbed my eyes. I slipped the rap sheet under the mattress, slipped under the covers and turned off the light.

I swore an oath to the night.

"Sly Barett, if the CIA doesn't get you, the Artful Dodger will."

* * *

The next morning, Bob drove me to New York. We spoke little.

He pulled up to the orphanage. We sat in the car for an awkward moment.

"What about my SpyPhone?" I asked.

He handed me a single, button-sized earbud. "Just this. Keep it in your pocket at all times. It automatically activates when you stick it in your ear. It'll call a secure line at headquarters. It should work in most parts of the city. The signal could be traced by Pharaoh, so use it *only* in emergency."

He reached into his pocket and handed me an old , dirty quarter.

I turned it in my hands, inspecting it. "What's this?"

"Your tracking device. It's built into the quarter. It's stained to identify it from a real one." I slipped it into my wallet.

He tried a lame joke to lighten the tension. "Just don't use it to make a phone call, okay? Heh, heh."

I forced myself to laugh. "Yeah, right."

We fumbled through an awkward goodbye. He offered his hand. After a moment's hesitation, I shook it. I got out.

I turned away so he couldn't see my eyes cloud up.

He drove off.

Doug's familiar voice called from the third story window.

"Hey, psycho! Your brain all fixed up now? Did they give you a la-*brat*-omy?"

I wagged a finger at him. "Better sleep with one eye open, pal. They turned me into a crazed killer now."

With the tip of my skateboard, I hooked the bottom of the fire escape ladder and pulled it down to the street. Grinning from ear to ear, I clambered up the rusty stairway to the third floor, my old home. As much as I hated the place, it felt great to be back with the old crew again.

Doug stepped away from the window and I slipped inside.

The orphanage was just the way I'd left it. Except no Randy. I looked to his bunk. Sheets, blanket and pillow all lay neatly stacked in the center of the empty cot.

I looked at Doug. "Where's Randy?"

Eyes downcast, Doug said, "Sent to Juvy, man."

"But he always told me on the phone that they couldn't make the charges stick."

"He didn't want you to worry about him."

I plopped down on Randy's cot. The rusty springs squeaked in protest. "What did he get?"

"Grand Theft Auto and Interstate Transport of a stolen vehicle. He won't get out till he turns eighteen."

I placed my hands over my eyes and groaned. "He'll wither and die in that place."

"So what about you?" Doug asked. "Back for good? Done with your testing?"

I shrugged. "We'll see."

I talked to Doug and the others for awhile, lying through my teeth about the 'psych experiment'.

*   *   *

The weeks dragged on; no sign of Pharaoh. My spirits sank from lack of action. I found myself missing Randy—and Bob—more and more.

Sometimes, milling about the neighborhood, I spotted the fake bodyguard, nearly always Bob. It took all my will power to turn away.

I was slowly going stir crazy. Somehow, I *had* to talk to him, see if we could work things out after all this blew over. But I wasn't even allowed to acknowledge his presence. But, as Dad used to say, time is a prisoner's best friend. After racking my brain, I devised a devious plan.

Doug and I took a train into town, then skateboarded from Grand Central station to a mall. We caught an early matinee. The theater was nearly empty, I was happy to see. The perfect place to meet Bob secretly, I figured.

As expected, Bob followed us in. He sat somewhere towards the back.

The lights dimmed. The movie started. After a few minutes, I glanced back.

Bob was gone.

By the flickering light of the movie, I searched each face in the theater. No trace of him. A chill ran up my spine. He would never abandon his post, unless . . . .

Here it comes, I thought.

Doug nudged me. "Hey, you gonna watch the flick or what?"

"Uh, thought I saw some cute chicks back there. Hey, I'm gonna go buy some popcorn. Tell me what happens." I grabbed my board and ran up the aisle.

I checked the restroom, just in case. "Bob?" I called, entering. No answer. Crouching low, I walked down the aisle and checked beneath each toilet stall for a pair of feet.

Behind me I heard, "Hey, Dodger."

I stood and turned. And froze. Scarface!

In his hand he held a spyPhone. "Say, this tracking device works pretty good," he said. "But you still owe me my old phone. And a little payback, too." He dropped the phone into a pocket and stepped toward me.

I shrank back. My elbow bumped against the cold, brick wall.

He advanced. His hand slipped inside his overcoat. Out came a pistol and silencer. He narrowed his eyes.

"You're more trouble than you're worth, boy," he growled. He chambered a round and took aim. "Compliments of the Pharaoh."

I whipped my board around and back-handed his gun away. The pistol fired with a *pop!* Flecks of concrete exploded at my feet. Whirling the skateboard back with a home run swing, I bashed his arm.

Scarface screamed in pain and fell to the floor.

I sprinted out the theater and into the mall, my heart racing faster than my feet. My mind raced as well. Scarface had tried, not to kidnap me, but kill me. And without 1A clearance for the discreet transponder code frequency, how could *he* track my secret bug?

I hopped on the board and skated fast to the escalator leading down to the lower level.

I glanced behind. Scarface emerged from the theater and staggered after me. Holstering his gun, he spoke into his earpiece.

I reached the top of the crowded escalator.

Halfway down, I heard a commotion below. A henchman bullied his way up the mobile steps. I looked back up. Scarface reached the top.

I glanced over the side. Long drop. Taking a deep breath, I dove over the opposite side, onto the smooth steel ramp between the up and down escalators. Belly flopping onto the skateboard, I rode down head first. The man grabbed for me, but too late.

"Whoa," I cried, accelerating out of control. At the bottom I flew off and crashed into a mother and daughter. They toppled to the ground like milk bottles in a carnival game. I hopped on the board and gave them a sympathetic shrug.

"Sorry," I said, pushing off.

I glanced behind. Pharaoh's men ran down the steps toward me, knocking people every which way. I skated through the mall, weaving around shoppers like they were slalom cones. I rounded a corner and skidded to a halt. Three henchmen raced toward me, a spyPhone in the leader's hand. I doubled back.

Tracker, I thought. Had to ditch the tracker. But I had no time.

Scarface stood next to the fountain in the center of the mall, bracing to snatch me as I passed. Swerving, I tried to fake him out. But on the smooth tile floor I could barely maneuver.

I crouched low, then plowed into him. He flew backward and plunged into the fountain. I fell off, grabbing the fountain's edge to keep from getting dunked.

I shook my head, dazed.

A lady screamed. People stared in shock. Looking like a cat dunked in the bath, and with a look of murder in his eyes, Scarface stood and drew his gun.

Time to move on. I skated fast toward the exit.

I raced through the double glass doors into the underground parking garage, and slammed into a kid on a bicycle. We crashed to the ground.

A big black Cadillac skidded to the curb a few feet away. Two more thugs jumped out.

I needed something faster than a skateboard. Springing to my feet, I grabbed the kid's bike and said, "Young man, in the name of national security, I am hereby liberating your transportation." I sped off.

The spies jumped back in their Cadillac. Scarface joined them. They peeled out.

I weaved through the packed parking lot. The Cadillac squealed into my row, tires angrily spitting rubber. I sailed between two parked cars into another lane. They roared up the aisle and whipped into the next row to cut me off. I glided between another row to escape. The pattern continued as I switched rows each time they caught up.

I was more maneuverable, but they were faster. And I was tiring quickly.

I crouched down between the handle bars to hide. But the deception worked both ways; I couldn't see them, either. After a moment, I peeked above the car tops and searched right, left, behind. Nothing. I neared the end of the lane.

The Cadillac screeched around the corner. I kicked the bike sideways and skidded to a stop. The driver gunned it. I recovered and pedaled up the aisle, nearly out of breath.

A beat up Camry backed out ahead. He shifted and pulled forward. I swerved around him and passed.

The Cadillac sped up to the Camry, then tailgated him in impatience. As I reached the front of the Camry, I cut sharp in front of him. He panicked and slammed on his brakes. The Cadillac rammed into him. A symphony of screeching metal and shattering glass filled my ears.

I circled around and back to the boy. He stared in disbelief, chin nearly dropped to the pavement. I laid the bike at his feet and pounced back on my board.

From my wallet I dug out the quarter tracker bug. I flipped him the coin. "Thanks, son. Your country is grateful for your service. And none of this ever happened."

Nodding absentmindedly, he caught the quarter, face still blank in amazement.

I pushed off and raced away. The henchmen jumped out of the Cadillac but stood there helpless, too far away to catch up.

I set out for the orphanage, skating down back alleys to the subway and constantly glancing over my shoulder.

Once on the moving train, I figured it was safe enough to call Cole on the emergency phone. I stuck the spongy button in my ear, and immediately heard the scratchy signal connect.

"Secure scrambled line, beta one six," said a gruff voice. "Code in."

"Er . . . Artful Dodger, november six two zero alpha whiskey."

"Code confirmed. Go for King Cole."

"Cole," I stammered, "Scarface tried to kill me—"

A lady across the aisle from me gasped in alarm, eyes wide with fear. I must have sounded to her like a typical subway loony spouting gibberish. I moved down the aisle and out of earshot from the other passengers.

"I know all about the attempted assassination," Cole answered calmly. "Don't worry, Dodger. Things are being taken care of. A man named Thomas will pick you up out in front of the orphanage in one hour. His code phrase will be, 'Nice day for water skiing'. Your response shall be, 'I'd rather go snow skiing in New Zealand'."

"Okay. But do you think it's safe there?"

"Our men have it well cased. Have you told any of your orphan friends about 'The Company'?"

"Of course not."

"Good. Don't."

"Hey, is Bob—er, uh, Fagin, safe?"

"Can't explain now. King Cole out."

Dejected, I slipped the earbud into my pocket. I prayed Pharaoh hadn't taken Bob out, too. Once back at the orphanage, I stretched out on my cot for a breather.

Doug returned from the movie. He punched my arm.

"Hey numbnuts, why'd you ditch me?"

I looked up at him. "Look, I—I can't tell you. I've gotta go somewhere, okay? I'll explain it all when I get back."

He shrugged. "Whatever. You didn't miss nothin'. The movie sucked anyway."

After the hour was up, I hit the street. Overcast clouds pressed down on the city. A light drizzle settled on my shoulders.

"Mr. Dodger?" a voice called from behind.

I turned. A tall, clean-shaven man in a chauffeur's cap smiled back.

"My name is Thomas. Nice day for waterskiing."

"Umm, I'd rather go snow skiing in New Zealand."

Thomas smiled. "Follow me." He grabbed my backpack and board and tossed them in the trunk of a shiny black limousine parked by the curb.

I didn't budge. Though he'd passed the test, after the chase at the mall I wasn't about to trust anyone.

I held up a finger. "Um, excuse me. Who sent you?"

He stopped and turned. His smile remained fixed, as if stuck on with Elmer's glue. With his free hand, he reached beneath his uniform coat. I tensed. But instead of a pistol, he pulled out a note. I took it and read.

To: Dodger

Fm: King Cole
Proceed with Thomas immediately. No questions asked.

I saw Cole's signature scrawled at the bottom, along with his secret code number designated to me and Bob. Whoever this Thomas guy was, he had to be legit. Or he'd gone pretty far to make it look that way.

He opened the limo's rear door and held out a hand in invitation.

A voice from above yelled, "Justin!"

I looked up to see Doug's face poking from the third story window. Several other orphans strained around him to catch a glimpse of my high class transport.

"You're a bum," Doug shouted.

I spread my hands wide and grinned wider. "Dream on, guys!" I called. I waved goodbye, then hopped in.

Thomas fired up the limo and pulled away.

I knocked on the privacy window that separated us. The smoky glass hummed down.

"Yes, Mr. Dodger?" Thomas asked, peering in the rear view mirror.

"Is, um, Fagin safe?"

"Enjoy the ride, sir." The dark screen zipped back up.

I'd never been in a limo before, and for the long drive to headquarters I intended to make the best of it. I switched on the TV. From the wet bar I poured a glass of Coke and root beer on the rocks and sat back. I flipped through the channels, sipped my drink and tried hard not to think about Bob.

After crossing the Holland tunnel and entering New Jersey, Thomas took a wrong turn. I tensed a minute, then relaxed, recalling my training. While driving somewhere secret, agents always doubled back and turned wrong to confuse and shake off the bad guys.

But then he pulled off the expressway and into a deserted section of boat docks by the Hudson River. He turned down a small alley between two dilapidated warehouses. A large Greyhound charter bus faced us, blocking our exit.

The limo stopped. Thomas rolled down the smokey glass window and said, "End of the line, Mr. Dodger."

My eyes widened at the phrase. But then he stepped out and obediently grabbed my gear from the trunk.

I got out. A heavy fog settled over me. The limo sped away into the mist.

With a hiss, the bus door opened. Cole emerged, followed closely by Hoffman. A soft breeze played at their raincoat tails; a light mist settled on their shoulders.

"Good afternoon, Justin," Cole greeted.

I got the feeling this wouldn't turn out to be the "good" afternoon he promised.

"Is Bob safe?" I blurted.

Cole held up a hand. "We found him unconscious in the theater, chloroformed. He's fine."

"But you're not," Max Hoffman added. I cocked my head in question. His wizard's grin grew wider. "On the news later today you'll hear about the death of Master Justice Malcomb Reed."

"What?" I glanced right and left, looking for an escape.

Cole raised a hand. "Settle down, son. No one's going to hurt you. We're faking your death. Pharaoh apparently thinks you know too much. He no longer wants you alive. He wants you silenced."

"So, we're silencing you for him," Hoffman said.

Cole took off his specs and stepped forward. "Son, it's time to level with you. I'm afraid I have some bad news. Several years ago, your father worked for us."

My mouth dropped open. "For the CIA?"

"Yes. Freelance stuff. An odd job here and there, in conjunction with the Air Force. His last job for us was in Afghanistan."

I recalled the *Rubber Soul* file from Bob's study, and the spy who'd cracked the case.

"Blue Jay. My dad was Agent Blue Jay."

Cole nodded.

"So he's a hero," I thought aloud.

Cole and Hoffman exchanged glances. Cole said, "Not exactly, son. Your father helped Pharaoh set up *Rubber Soul*."

"What?" I exclaimed.

Hoffman stared straight in my eyes and said, "Then Agent Blue Jay double-crossed Pharaoh, stole his drug money, and blew the whistle on him."

I froze, unable to think straight. Then anger gushed through. I pounded a fist on the bus door. Jabbing a finger at Hoffman, I said through clenched teeth, "There is no way, *no way*, that my dad could *possibly* be a drug smuggler."

Hoffman's eyes seemed to dare me to attack.

"Sit down, Justin," Cole said, soft but stern. I slumped onto the steps of the bus entrance. "I'm sorry, son, truly I am. But the evidence points otherwise. We had no idea of his guilt at the time, until the Pharaoh ordered him killed."

I sat in silence, thinking. Dad had always talked like he had my money for college but never did. Was it because he—? No way. No freakin' way. Slowly I looked up at them. It seemed like it took every ounce of energy in my body to do so. "What happens to me now?" I asked dejectedly.

"You start a new life," Cole said cheerfully. I didn't share his feelings. "You see, in about half an hour, that limousine you were just in will blow up. Car bomb, presumably Mafia. Since several witnesses saw you enter the limo, we'll have no trouble proving that you're dead. And you and Thomas will both get a second chance at life."

I recalled Doug and the orphans waving goodbye. They would think—

My guts churned. My head swam. The deep fog pressed heavy on my shoulders.

Cole pointed a finger at me. "Justin, you must never, *ever* see your old friends again. To do so would bring extreme risk to you. And them."

"Randy and Doug? Glen and Joya? Not even Bob?"

Hoffman said, "After what happened, Robert Cheney is now our main suspect."

"Bob, the Pharaoh? *Impossible!*" I stood and stepped toward them. I remembered all the things Bob had done for me. And I recalled his son, dead from a drug o.d. Could Bob really be the cold-hearted killer and drug smuggler they claimed? I couldn't believe it. "But—you said he got knocked out in the theater."

Hoffman shrugged. "Probably arranged that to divert suspicion. I would have expected Pharaoh to eliminate him."

Never in my life had I felt so low. Dad, accused of drug smuggling. Bob, a suspected traitor and killer. And all my friends thinking I died in a car bomb. My lips trembled, and curled into a frown. My legs felt wobbly. I collapsed onto the steps. I buried my face in my hands and cried.

After a few minutes, I felt a nudge. Cole offered a handkerchief. I took it and blew my nose.

He lay a hand on my shoulder. "Bob may still be innocent, you understand. I admit the evidence is sketchy at best, but as you know, in this business it always is. Nevertheless, we'll be watching him closely from now on."

I looked up from the hanky. "So where are you sending me now?"

"A place where you have longed to go for years," he said with false cheerfulness. "Los Angeles. Close to your parents' graves at last."

Hoffman pulled out a document and handed it to me. "Here's your new birth certificate, with your new name on it."

I read it. And crinkled my nose in disgust.

"Percival Brimley?" I choked on the name like it was a gulp of sour milk. "You can't be serious."

Cole shrugged. "Sorry about that. Random computer name. At least you're the same age, except the birth date's a few weeks off."

I looked over the paper at them. "Same age? Does that mean I go—"

"To an orphanage. That's the law, son."

"Law," I spat. Slapping the certificate, I stood and stepped boldly toward them. Not a very intimidating move coming from a kid, I know, but my rage made me feel ten feet tall. "Let me tell you two about law. It was *illegal* for you to con me into this. And don't b.s. about protecting me. You should have sent me to the Witness Protection Program from the start, just like Bob said. But instead you *tricked* me into volunteering, to expose me to your *Rubber Soul* suspects. And—and all my *Lenin Star* instructors, they were suspects, too, weren't they?"

I stopped, and stared blankly ahead as a revelation hit. *"Lenin Star,"* I thought aloud, *"Rubber Soul* . . . . Your operation wasn't *Lenin Star* at all, was it? It was *'Lennon Starr'*. John *Lennon* and Ringo *Starr*, two of the Beatles who made the album, *Rubber Soul*. And you'd named it that long before I ever came along. You two set it up just for *me*!"

Cole and Hoffman exchanged glances; I'd guessed right.

Why hadn't I figured it out before? I'd been so blind with excitement at playing spy games, I never saw the connection. Rage burned so furiously within me I could hardly see straight. I shook the birth certificate in Hoffman's face.

"You'd planned to use me as bait from the *beginning*!"

He met my gaze with a poker face. His arms remained crossed, relaxed, as if protected by a glass wall. "Nice of you to come up with the idea for us. Took the heat off selling it."

Cole said evenly, "You will be bused to headquarters. Once at Langley, you will debrief. Then on to Los Angeles. An agent will escort you, just to make sure there's no trouble. He won't know who you are—or, rather, were. Only that it is imperative that you make it safely to L.A. Tell your new friends that you were simply transferred from New York to be close to your parents' graves."

Hoffman signaled the driver. The bus rumbled to life.

Cole said coldly, "Good day, Percival Brimley. Your country is grateful for your service."

Hoffman wagged a finger. "And none of this ever happened."

I trudged up the steps. With a wretched hiss, the bus doors closed.

Closed on my old life.

CHAPTER 7: CARLOS HOLDS THE KEY

I turned to my escort, a tall, skinny, dorky-looking guy with ears bigger than his whole head. He straightened his tie, patted down his black suit, and smiled a big, geeky grin. He shook my hand as if it was a can of paint.

"You're Percival Brimley, right?" he asked. "Im Agent Bozowski. "Vernon Bozowski. You can call me Vern." He cupped his hand to his mouth and bellowed, "All aboard the CIA Express!" He looked down at my stuff. "Hey, radical skateboard, *dude*."

I rolled my eyes and stomped to the back. Vern followed on my heels.

I plopped down on a seat; I didn't offer him the one next to me. He leaned on the arm rest across the aisle, slapped his knees and smiled.

Wringing his hands he said, "Well, Percival, we've got the entire bus to ourselves for the whole trip. Isn't that *swell*? But, I'm not s'posed to ask any questions and you're not s'posed to give any answers, so I guess we have to talk about the weather all the way, huh? Heh, heh. And, no cells or wifi allowed either, I'm afraid. Boss's orders. But hey, we got plenty of neat stuff to do. Cards, magazines, we even got Monopoly. You like Monopoly, Percival? I love Monopoly."

"Ungh," I growled. I wasn't quite in the talkative mood.

"There's a coupla cots to sleep on, a bathroom in back and a fridge full of snacks and drinks. Isn't that *swell*?" He poked me in the belly. "But no beer, 'kay dude? Heh, heh."

We drove, for how long I didn't know, to who knows where I didn't care. I just sat and gazed out the window, unable to think of anything but grief.

We joined the Jersey Turnpike and crept southward in heavy traffic. Vern pointed to and explained each and every sight.

"Yeah, I grew up out here," he rambled. "Swell place, eh Percival? Where are you from, anyway? Oops, don't ask, don't tell, right? Jeez, can you believe this rush hour traffic? We could get out and walk faster."

He seemed content to do all the talking, so I tuned him out and thought about the conversation with Cole and Hoffman.

Afghanistan. Dad's last station in the military. I remembered his stories well. Memories flooded back. I recalled a funny thing that happened when he moved back to New York. As soon as he got Stateside, he ordered a headstone for his grave marker. I always figured some smooth New York operator conned him. And I gave him no end of grief for it, teasing him about New York shysters. But now I understood why he worried about it.

Maybe Dad really did work for CIA. Maybe he knew more about the smuggling ring than he let on. But knowingly take part? Not a chance. I had to prove his innocence. I couldn't go through life without clearing his name. And Bob's name, too, if he was innocent. Pharaoh would pay. Along with his henchman Sly. Someone had to know. Someone close to Dad in—

That was it! Sgt. Carlos Martinez, Dad's and my fishing buddy in Panama. Their unit's next assignment had been Afghanistan.

As far as I knew, Carlos and his family still lived in Baltimore. And the CIA Express would pass right through the city enroute to headquarters.

One way or another, I was getting off this bus in Baltimore. But first I had to escape from my mobile prison and its guard, Bozowski the Clown.

I let CIA training take over, searching for an escape route, a diversion, a plan. I said to myself, "Okay Artful Dodger, master of evasion, how do you give a fully trained CIA agent the slip and escape a moving bus?"

We trundled past Trenton and Philadelphia and approached Baltimore. I had to do it now. But do what? Try as I might, I came up blank. In the rush hour traffic, we circled around the outskirts of town at a skateboard's pace.

Yes, a skateboard's pace . . . . The gears began to churn in my head.

Vern rambled on about this sight and that, like a tour guide bucking for a tip.

"And on our right, we have Oriole Park at Camden Yards, home of the Baltimore Orioles. Ever go to a pro ball game, Percival?"

"Yeah." I remembered the double-header, the kidnappers in the bathroom, the nausea I felt after nearly shooting Scarface. An idea hit.

I held my head and groaned. "Gee, Vern. Bus rides don't sit too *swell* with my stomach. You think you could fetch me a pop or something?"

"Oh, sure *dude*."

He trotted to the refrigerator and brought back a cola and box of soda crackers. He sat back on the arm rest and felt my forehead like a worried mother.

"You okay, buddy?"

"I think I'm gonna be sick."

I chomped up a cracker, but didn't swallow it. I sucked in a huge gulp of pop, then, setting the can down in a seat, swished the soda and crumbs around in my mouth.

"Hey, maybe you'd better go the bathroom."

I nodded. Then blew chunks.

"Blech," I cried, spewing the crumb-filled soda into his lap.

"What the—" He jumped up, hands raised in surprise.

I doubled over, hiding the wallet and spyPhone I'd picked off him during the diversion. He scurried up the aisle for a towel, his back turned, absorbed in wiping the fake barf from his pants.

"I'll be in the john," I called, grabbing my skateboard and backpack and running to the rear of the bus. I slipped inside the bathroom.

The cramped quarters left little room for my gear, but I didn't plan on staying long.

I looked up. Printed in big red letters on the ceiling of the stall were the words that I'd prayed to see.

Escape Hatch. Use Only in Emergency.

I pulled out all Vern's cash from his wallet. On his SpyPhone, I wrote a note.

> Dear Vern,
> Sorry I couldn't hang around. It's been swell, dude.
> I.O.U. $148.00.
> Sincerely,
> Percival Brimley
> (aka The Artful Dodger)

I would have loved to take his phone with me, plugged in as it was to the CIA intranet. But it worked both ways, I knew; online, the CIA would track me down and capture me before I could say, "Vern Bozowski."

But I had a better idea. Punching the Record button on the touch screen, I imitated a few more loud and nasty pukes, then set it on continuous playback. Tossing it into the sink with his wallet, I strapped on my pack, stood on top of the toilet seat and popped the hatch. Air rushed by overhead. I tossed my board, upside down, out onto the roof.

Vern knocked. "Hey, Percival, you okay in there?"

"*Blech,*" blared the spyPhone, letting out a perfectly-timed gnarly barf. I couldn't help but snicker. Bending back down, I added, "I'm, okay Vern. Don't mind me. I'll be in here awhile, okay? Just go set up the Monopoly game and I'll be out in a— *Blech!*"

"Okay, bud. I'll even give you an extra $500 and the race car piece, 'kay dude? And if there's anything you need, let me know."

"Mm hmm. Thanks for the extra money. *Blech!*"

I pulled the emergency rope from its stowage compartment, tossed it out and clambered up, kicking off the toilet paper roll. Topside, I knelt on the roof and looked back. No cops. I hoped the driver of the Subaru behind us wasn't a CIA tail. His startled look said no.

We inched along in the traffic jam. Ten miles an hour, I figured. A sign ahead read, Caton Next Right. Never heard of the street. But it was my exit, I knew that.

I tossed the line over the back and wedged the skateboard between my body and the bus. Slowly, carefully, I slipped down the side using the skate as a dolly. My sneakers reached the rear bumper.

The exit approached. Gripping the escape rope, I crouched low. I swung out like Tarzan and jumped onto the board, swerving for a moment before catching my balance. I sailed down the off ramp, waving goodbye to the Subaru.

With a little luck, Vern would be miles away before he discovered my escape.

I coasted down the ramp, a long, shallow downhill ride. I casually slalomed to the bottom, taking the time to exercise my muscles, do a couple wheelies and enjoy the ride. The ramp sloped level as it merged with Caton Street, and my momentum carried me a few hundred feet on.

A group of kids gabbed on the sidewalk ahead. A sign behind them read, Seton Keough High School. Kids just getting out of summer school. The perfect place to blend in. I skated by. They all hushed and stared as I passed, but I just ignored them and skated on.

I held out my thumb to hitchhike. And lucked out. A guy in a Porsche peeled out from the parking lot across the street. He stopped and opened the door. I hopped in.

"Thanks."

"No problem," he answered, pulling away from the curb. He wore a white smock over a shirt and tie. I glanced back through the rear window and read the name of the building he had just left. St. Agnes Hospital.

"Oh, are you a doctor at Agnes?" I asked, trying to act like a local.

"Yes, I'm in residency," he answered with a healthy dose of pride. "Been here almost a year." He shifted and sped up. "So, where you headed?"

"Me? Oh, um, I'm just finishing summer school at Seton Keough, so I'm going to the, to the—" I motioned ahead, as if forgetting the word.

"McDonalds?"

"Yeah, that's it, the McDonalds. Up here on um, on um—"

"Wilkens?"

"Yeah, yeah. Wilkens. Sorry, my brain's kind of fried right now. I just had this big algebra test, you know?"

"Hey, I know the feeling. Algebra, huh?"

I nodded.

"You know, I went to Keough way back in the dark ages. Is old man Trevor still teaching algebra there?"

I bit my lip. "Um, I don't have him. But I think my friend does."

"Hmm."

I could tell he was reliving his high school glory days. This could get dangerous.

"How 'bout Miss Boldershack? Is that old prune still teaching English? Sure was a homely old maid. She must be retired by now."

"Oh, yeah, she's retired. Mm hmm." I felt a wave of relief as I saw the McDonalds up ahead.

"Of course, my favorite teacher was Buddy Barrows." He laughed as we pulled into the parking lot. "Lord, what a character. All beer belly and coke bottle glasses and that horrible breath. Is he still there?"

He stopped. I opened the door and jumped out. I couldn't resist pulling his leg.

"Nah, he ain't there any more. He married Miss Boldershack and they joined the Hari Krishnas. Thanks for the ride!"

He stared back, dumbfounded. I closed the door and headed into the restaurant, snickering.

I held up the good doctor's phone, palmed from the armrest of his Porsche. As I pulled a list of phone numbers from my wallet, a photo tumbled to the floor. I picked it up. Taken in a photo booth at the fair, it was a goofy shot of Bob and me. I was sticking my tongue out while Bob pushed up his nose with his thumb. As I gazed at the picture, a tear found its way into the corner of each eye.

I said to his photo, "You can't be guilty."

"Huh?" a guy asked as he passed by me and into the john.

"Oh, nothin'."

I put Bob's photo away and tapped Carlos's number. I hoped it was still good. The phone rang twice and a kid answered. Carlos's son Ricky, I could tell. But I avoided calling him by name.

"*Bueno*—hello," he said.

"*Hola*—hi," I answered in Spanish. "Um, can you get your dad on the phone?"

"*Uno momento, por favor*—One moment please."

After a minute, Carlos got on.

"Hello?"

"Hello." I paused, unable to think of what to say.

"Who is this?"

"This is your fishin' buddy. No names over the phone, please."

"*Madre de Dios*—Mother of God! How are you?"

"I'm afraid I'm—I'm in trouble."

"With whom? The law? Did you run away again?"

"Yes to both. But it's way, *way* worse than that." I searched for words. "*Amigo*, I need to know something. Was Dad involved with, you know, a certain government 'company' out in the Middle East?"

The line went silent. For a moment I feared someone had disconnected us. Then I heard him take a deep sigh.

"I thought you might ask that some day," he said heavily. "Where are you?"

"In town. Can you pick me up?"

"You bet. Where?"

I told him. I said I'd be hiding in the bathroom stall. One thing I'd learned from spy school, it paid to be paranoid.

"I'll be there in half an hour," he replied. "I have something for you from your dad."

"*What*?" I exclaimed, nearly dropping the phone.

"Not over an open line."

"Right." I hung up and stared at the phone.

Something for me from Dad.

After munching a couple burgers, I hid in the john. I sat on the porcelain throne and read *Oliver*, trying to keep my mind off that little something from Dad.

After a while, I heard a knock.

"Justin?" Carlos's familiar voice called.

Heart pounding, I burst from the stall.

He'd shaved off his bushy mustache, and his receding black hair was sprouting more than a few grays. But it was him.

I hugged him. "It's great to see you."

"Likewise," he said, grinning a grin that could light all the city.

He held me at arm's length.

"Boy, have you grown. And look at those muscles!"

I poked his beer belly. "You've grown too. But sideways!"

He mussed my hair. "Aww, still the smart-a, hmm?"

I glanced around the room. "We'd better make tracks."

We walked through the burger joint. Unable to talk business in the open, I used the chance to catch up with his life.

"So, what have you been up to?" I asked. "I mean, besides being a baby factory?"

He laughed. "Security guard. Can you believe it? A damned night security guard. I still make a few extra bucks tinkering with cars like you and me and your dad used to do down in Panama, though."

We hopped in his ancient, rusty blue Dodge Coronet.

"See you haven't changed your style," I teased.

"You should talk, you delinquent," he shot back. He started up. "Anyway, my good man *Jesus Christos* provides for us well enough. He fingered a gold crucifix that hung from a chain around his neck. "Like it?" I nodded. "Sally's mother made it for me. Been good luck ever since."

I admired the handiwork. "Nice."

We pulled into traffic.

I couldn't wait to hear about that Something from Dad.

"So, what do you have for me?"

Carlos shook his head. "Un unh, *señor*. First let's hear your story. I want to hear just what you know."

"Jeez, you sound like one of them." I fell silent. There was too much to say, and I didn't know where to start. Finally, I took a deep breath. "Carlos, the CIA trained me like an agent, then used me as bait to try and capture Dad's killer."

He shot a surprised glance at me. "*You?*" I nodded. He eyed me skeptically. "Justin, you sure you're not just making this up are you? To be like your dad or something?"

I reached into my jacket pocket and produced the forged birth certificate. He read the fake name. And bellowed.

"*Percival Brimley?*"

"Shut up or I'll deck ya," I growled.

"Sorry." He suppressed his laugh. A little.

I told him the entire story, including the accusations Cole had made about Dad.

We reached his home, inside an old barrio row house. Three of his kids skipped rope in front of the stoops crumbling concrete steps. We greeted them, then entered and climbed the rickety stairs to his third story apartment.

"Justin, how are you?" his wife Sally asked as we walked in. She gave me a hug, then shooed the two youngest kids away to leave Carlos and me alone.

"Beer?" Carlos asked. I shook my head no. "Good, I wasn't gonna give you one anyway." He pulled a Bud from the refrigerator and sat down in a dark brown, overstuffed chair patched with duct tape. I sat on the frayed couch. Slowly, his cheery bright smile darkened to a deadly scowl. He popped the top and swigged, then sat silent. After a long moment, he looked me square in the eyes and spoke.

"Your dad did *not* smuggle drugs."

I sat back, the world lifting from my shoulders. I'd known it all along, but to hear it from someone who had been there made all the difference.

After a long, reflective moment, Carlos began his story.

"One day in Kabul, your dad and I were loading crates onto an Air Force C-141 transport plane bound for the States, transferring them from a plane that had come in from Tillman FOB—that means Forward Operating Base."

"I know."

"While carrying one, I tripped on the grating inside the aircraft and we dropped the box to the floor. It broke open and a brown powder spilled out. Opium.

"Malcomb grew furious, knowing that we and the Air Force had been duped into helping a drug smuggling operation. He insisted on reporting it. I tried to talk him out of it, afraid for our lives if the wrong people discovered what we'd seen. But to him that crate of drugs represented a personal threat to you. So he went."

Carlos took another swig and shrugged. "That was it. He retired from the Air Force a few months later to take care of you. I didn't hear any more about it." He leaned forward and stared me in the eyes.

"Until Malcomb's letter arrived in the mail," he said gravely. He set the beer down on the coffee table and stood. "In it, he confessed to me that he'd been working for CIA all along, but never knew anything about the drug smuggling."

Carlos walked over to a book shelf. "He asked me to give this to you if anything suspicious ever happened to him." He reached behind a stack of books and pulled out a manila envelope, addressed to me in Dad's handwriting. He handed it over.

"For your own good, Justin, and I hope you forgive me for this, I never sent it to you after his death. I never opened it either, 'cause I know what it is. It's a Pandora's Box, *amigo*. I'm warning you: whatever's in that envelope, you don't want no part of it."

Glaring into his eyes, I ripped away the yellowed tape. "I'm already part of it."

I opened the envelope flap. Out fell a letter. And a key.

I picked up the key and studied it. A gold Master, serial number p1505. The same one Scarface had been looking for. I sat forward on the couch and read the message, scrawled in my father's handwriting.

Dear Justin,

If you are reading this letter, it means something has happened to me, and I am afraid an explanation is in order. I tried to keep this secret, as it did not concern you. Working for the CIA was for the good of the country, I believed, and that is why I did it.

On my final mission, as Carlos will tell you, I discovered an illegal smuggling operation. I investigated the matter and came up with nothing. Nothing, that is, except a communiqué which calls the smuggling operation Rubber Soul and its coordinator, Pharaoh. I never did discover his real name.

Pharaoh shipped drugs to America under the CIA's nose, and channeled the profits into a numbered bank account in the Bahamas. How much money, I don't know. But I am sure it runs in the millions.

In my fury, I stole the key required to open the account. I thought I could ruin his operation and profit at the same time. But as I contemplated the gravity of what I had done, I became frightened and sat on the information instead.

If the smugglers really have caught up to me, then they can't be far behind you. In that case, I advise you to turn this letter and the key over to the FBI for investigation. Beware of the Pharaoh.

I love you and always have. I am sorry I failed you. Sayonara.

Your father,

Malcomb

P.S. Come visit me, and I shall give you the key to Rubber Soul.

I remained motionless, staring at his signature. My eyes grew cloudy. Tears drip-dripped like a leaky faucet onto the page.

Carlos bent forward and reached for the letter.

"May I?" he asked.

Head hung low, I held it out.

"Come visit me and I shall give you the key to *Rubber Soul*," Carlos quoted as he finished. He pointed to the brass latchkey in my hand. "But I thought that was the key. I wonder what he means by—It doesn't matter, Justin. Do what he says. Give the key to the FBI and tell them your story."

"They'll never believe it."

"Oh, yes they will. With that birth certificate and this key, they have to."

"But nothing will be done. They'll meet a brick wall with the CIA. Cole will say I stole the stuff or something. Pharaoh will go free. And Bob will be branded a traitor and Dad a drug smuggler." I wiped away the tears with my sleeve.

The phone rang. Carlos picked up. He looked sharply at me, and stared into my eyes as he spoke. "Why, hello Mrs. Kraumas. Yes, I remember you from Justin's orphanage. How is the young man these days? Doing his studies, I hope? Oh my God, that's *awful*! How terrible." He paused while Kraut yakked away. "Well, thank you for calling, Mrs. Kraumas. Please call me back with the funeral arrangements. You take care of yourself. God bless you, ma'am." He hung up. "It's official, Justin. You're dead."

I took a deep sigh. "Oh, man. All my friends think I'm history."

"Go to the Feds, Justin," he urged gently.

But I couldn't. Not yet. I needed evidence, evidence of Bob's innocence and Pharaoh's identity. I sat for a long time, thinking. I forced myself to bury the pain and come up with a plan.

Cole and Hoffman had created *Lenin Star* to flush out the Pharaoh. And flush he did, almost killing me. Pharaoh had known about Bob *and* the other CIA tail, and had even known the frequency and transponder code of my tracker bug. That meant he had to be someone close on the case, perhaps someone I'd met during training. If I could flush him, I was sure to recognize him. I knew what had to be done.

I looked up. "I have a lead."

Carlos cocked his head sideways and narrowed his eyes. "What lead?"

"I think I know how to find Dad's killer, Sly Barett. He can lead me to Pharaoh."

"And what if this Pharaoh guy really is Bob?"

"I can't believe that."

"But if he is?"

I sighed. "I don't know. He was so good to me. Maybe too good. I have to find out, one way or another. Look, if nothing comes of it, I'll go to the FBI. I Promise." I bit my lip. "Carlos, I could use your help. It might involve guns."

He looked at me a long time, his expression slowly drooping. Finally, he shook his head and sighed.

"I'm sorry, Justin, I can't. I mean, it's not that I don't want to. I owe Malcomb my life." He looked at the floor. "There was this incident on base once . . . ." He stopped and looked back up at me. "I would if I were single, Justin. You know that. But the wife and kids. What would become of them if anything happened to me?"

I held up my hand. "You're right, Carlos. It's my fight. I shouldn't have asked."

"If there's anything I can do, just name it."

"Look, I gotta move fast. First I have to make a secret visit to Washington. Can you drive me down to D.C., tonight?"

"Hmm. I'll have to call in sick. But, sure."

"Then I'm gonna need you to buy me a plane ticket up to New York. I don't know when I can pay you back."

"You can pay me back by staying alive, Justin. But don't you think you'd better avoid being seen in public for awhile?"

"I'll take the chance." I straightened, and thumped my chest in mock pride. "Besides, you're lookin' at a CIA-trained escape artist!"

The aromatic smell of red chilies and beans wafted out to the living room. I inhaled deeply.

Carlos said, "Let's eat dinner first, Justin. And you can catch a few winks on the couch before we leave."

"Thanks," I replied. "And it *is* great to see you. Even under these circumstances."

I had a great time visiting the family and playing with his kids. Finally, Carlos and I saw them off to bed and we prepared for the trip.

At an all night supermarket, Carlos bought some extra clothes for me. He also picked up some blond hair dye to complete my disguise. Sally cut my long hair into a crew cut, then I showered with the shampoo coloring. Upon seeing my bleached, butchered locks in the mirror, I winced.

Carlos laughed. "Hmm, I think you need some Groucho glasses, too. You know, those ones with the plastic nose and mustache."

I rolled my eyes. "Oh yeah, right. That'll help me blend."

To complete the disguise, he gave me a duffel bag in which to hide my skateboard and backpack.

We drove down past D.C. to McClean, a quick couple hours at that time of night. Carlos dropped me off near Bob's back yard.

Bob was gone, I could tell. Avoiding all the CIA alarms, I snuck up and broke into the Locked Chamber and safe. The gun case and files were gone. I grabbed the spyPhone and bluetooth, a handful of listening bugs and trackers, and a few other gadgets from the box. Punching on the spyPhone, a greeting from Madge confirmed that my DNA and fake agent name still worked, though the CIA database was still off limits. To keep them from tracking me, I had her disable the online mode completely, then powered her down. I stuffed the gadgets into my backpack, and in a flash ran back to Carlos's getaway car.

By the time we reached Washington National Airport, the first glimmer of sun peeked from the horizon. We picked a commuter flight to La Guardia, the closest airport to my target. Saying I was his "dependent," Carlos bought a ticket for me under his son's name and escorted me to the gate, where I gave him a big farewell hug.

He handed me a couple hundred bucks. "Hey, Justin. Sorry I can't help."

"You've done more than enough. Really."

He pulled the gold chain and crucifix from around his neck and handed it to me. "For luck," he said.

I took it, then slid Dad's key, the one from his letter, onto the chain and hooked the whole thing around my neck.

Carlos shook my hand one last time.

"Let me know how it turns out *amigo*. And *vaya con Dios*— Go with God."

"*Gracias*." I waved and headed for the security line.

I sank into the seat cushion as the Canadair RJ Regional Jet raced down the runway, hurtling me toward New York.

And straight into enemy territory.

CHAPTER 8: GANG FIGHT

As the RJ squeaked down at La Guardia Airport, I jolted awake.

I fought off the urge to hole up at the orphanage. Way too dangerous. Besides, Doug and the gang had to keep thinking I was dead, or Pharaoh might find out.

I took a train to the lower end of Harlem and checked into a cheap hotel. Cheap meaning a dump, not low cost.

When you need a disguise, for Halloween or a secret mission, there's nothing better than a thrift shop. So I skated down to the nearest Goodwill store. I found exactly what I wanted, a dorky, flowery Hawaiian shirt and Bermuda tourist shorts. Grand total, $4.50. To complete the image, I picked up a camera at a pawn shop. Not a tiny pocket digital, but a big bulky one with a long lens, like the pros used to use. Old and battered, the thing still set me back thirty bucks.

In the hotel lobby I hung out with the, shall we say, *upper crust* of society. While shooting the breeze with the locals, I dropped a few casual questions about the Bones gang to scam more info on them. In the afternoon, I took a long *siesta* to prepare for the night's dirty deeds.

Darkness fell. Show time. I slipped on the disguise, took a deep breath and stepped out of the room. The camera swayed around my neck as I stole down the seedy hall toward the stairwell. The guy in the next room stood in his doorway, bouncing to the reggae-rap beat that pounded from his speakers. Upon seeing my outfit, he crinkled his bushy brows.

"Say dere brotha, whassup? You goin' to a costume party or someting?"

"Nope. Going fishin'."

With a mouth full of yellow teeth, he smiled back. "Mo' like you da bait."

"Wish me luck."

"Right. You'll need it."

At the street corner I ducked into the subway entrance. The hot, humid air of the underground mobile sardine cans hit me. The polyester Hawaiian shirt itched, and trapped the heat in. Sweat, as much from nerves as heat, trickled down my side. I slinked down the steps.

Flicking a token into the slot, I slid through the turnstile. A train roared into the station. Adrenaline kicked in and my heart beat in time with the *clack-clack* of the train cars. The train squealed to a halt.

I jumped on and took a side seat near the front of the car. I leaned back, closed my eyes and thought about the plan, about my IO—*Immediate Objective*—and *target*, trying to think in the terms taught in training.

My plan was simple. Get off near Sly Barett's gang territory in the Bronx. Once there, I knew there'd be no trouble finding trouble. With some of the Bones zombies.

We trundled through several stations, each stop closer to Sly country. I again closed my eyes and breathed deeply, to slow my heart and stop the adrenaline. I'd need the whole supply real soon, but not quite yet.

Trouble came before I wanted it.

The rear door slammed shut. I opened my eyes and looked up. Four teens, dressed in gang colors and obviously on the prowl, worked their way forward through the train, searching for marks. They'd been cussing and laughing when they first entered. But when they spotted me they grew silent, like a tomcat stalking a pigeon.

I had asked for it, and now I was getting it. But from the wrong gang, and in the wrong turf.

They sat in the middle of the car next to an exit, speaking in low mumbles. Each glanced my way a few too many times. Amateurs, but experienced. So, they planned to follow me out and hit me elsewhere. Better chance to trap me in a dark corner.

Though CIA had trained me to fight multiple opponents, the first rule of self-defense was always escape if possible. And, tell the truth, I'd never really tested my new skills in the real world; everybody had their limits, and I had no desire to try my luck with these toughies.

To keep them off guard, I played up the dumb tourist role. I widened my eyes and opened my mouth in wonderment. Pretending not to see them, I began reading all the advertisements above the windows of the car; something locals never do. I jumped from one side of the car to the other to look at each station. Each move kept them in sight out of the corner of my eye, in case they jumped the gun.

And speaking of guns, I *mental-frisked* each goon like Bob had taught me. I scanned the places a street thug would hide a weapon: inside pockets, socks, waistband under the jacket. Tough from this distance, but training paid off.

Bingo. One handgun, under the leader's belt, in back. Probably a .38 *Saturday Night Special*, but I couldn't be sure. No others. Plenty of switchblades though. Yep, way too much muscle and fire power for me to handle. Time to fly.

As the next stop approached, I stood and walked over to the window by the front exit door, acting like something had caught my eye. The train slowed. I pretended not to expect the sudden lurch, and, falling, grabbed the vertical handrail.

One gangster laughed, but was quickly silenced by an upheld hand from the leader. The four tensed as I approached the door, but relaxed as I began to snap photos through the window. I finished and sat down by the door.

I closed my eyes and rubbed them as if weary from a long day of sightseeing. Through my fingers I snuck a peek. They settled back in their seats.

Through the open, double sliding doors, a couple passengers filed in and out. Then the exit lay bare. I listened for the hiss of the door's air pressure system. Just a few more seconds, I figured. I ran my fingers across the vertical pole that stretched from floor to ceiling. Slowly I grasped it.

I heard the hiss, like a SCUBA diver exhaling. With lightning speed I stood and spun, pivoting around the pole to fling out between the closing doors. I slipped through sideways, nearly leaving a tennis shoe behind. The doors slammed shut.

"Hey," one gangster shouted. They jumped to their feet and lunged for the door. The train lurched and they toppled into each other like the Three Stooges. They slid by, staring at me in disbelief.

I grinned back and flipped them a gesture I knew they'd understand.

The tomcats had just seen the bird fly away.

While I waited for the next train, I fended off two beggars and a drunk who thought I should take a swig from the bottle in his brown paper bag. With my palm I pushed on his rancid coat to shoo him off, my nose crinkling at the foul smell of his breath. He stepped forward again for one more try, but my annoyed, *don't mess with me* street gaze stopped him cold. He took an unsteady step back and staggered away, mumbling to himself about kids these days, there's no respect and such.

Smiling, I boarded the next train. This really was a concrete jungle, where the predators quickly pounced on a lost animal. But communication between the local beasts was simple if one knew the lingo. I felt at home, even if my dorky outfit didn't.

I emerged from the subway to a not-so-well lit street in a not-so-well kept neighborhood. I started the lost tourist act again. Actually, it wasn't much of an act; I really was lost in this neighborhood.

I caught myself wishing for a weapon. Just that little Colt .380 hiding in my palm. Or at least a switchblade, still the weapon of choice among ghetto kids everywhere.

But weapons on a covert mission can cause more trouble than they prevent, Bob had taught me. If your enemy spots your armament, he'll be ready, and might even attack before you've maneuvered the situation to your best advantage.

I remembered Dad, too, and his stories from prison.

"*Anything* can be a weapon," he'd told me once, "the more ordinary and inconspicuous the object, the better. And believe me, those prisoners come up with some ingenious devices."

I relaxed, knowing I really was well armed.

I threw the line in the water and began to fish, once again using *me* as the lure.

Memories of fishing with Dad helped put my mind at ease. I recalled our outings to Point Camp in the California

Sierras, to the New York Catskills, down in Panama. Even my first ventures in Japan.

And, like real fishing, I had to be patient, it turned out. The mean streets actually seemed friendly. Several cop cars cruised by, and one even stopped.

He pulled up slowly and rolled down the window.

"Say there, buddy, you look lost."

I laughed, then answered in thick Bronx accent, "Nah, no problem, boss. Just goin' to a costume party. Down the street, you know?"

He chuckled in disbelief. "If you say so, pal." He drove off.

I walked on the edge of the sidewalk next to the street, avoiding the shadows that crowded each building and might hide a mugger. Besides, walking near the street exposed me to the stalkers of the night.

I rounded a corner and the skin on my neck tingled. There, halfway down the block, silhouetted by a street lamp, loomed two figures. One sat on a stoop leading up to a row house. The other stood on the sidewalk, one foot propped on a garbage can.

I scuffed my foot extra loud to get their attention, then glanced behind at the sidewalk as if a crack had caught me.

They perked up and gazed at me. The first kid stood and took a couple steps down to the sidewalk.

I stared wide-eyed at the tall buildings, glancing back and forth at each side of the street. When I was close enough for them to see my face—and for me to see their armament—I stopped, pulled out a map from my back pocket and scratched my head. I continued toward them. Twenty feet away, one of them spoke up.

"Hello. Uh, say, you need some help there, kid?" Sappy sweet, false politeness oozed from his words like jelly from a donut.

"Well, howdy," I answered, picking a nice flat Midwestern accent. That type gets a con thinking *sucker* quicker than any. I held up my map. "Say, think you guys can point me to the zoo? The Bronx Zoo? I'm not from around here, you see."

The two sharks circled, picking up the scent. Like the subway hoods, they were a little older and bigger than me. Both wore black and white ballcaps, backwards. When one gansta looked around to check for witnesses, I saw a skull and crossbones embroidered on the front. My heart skipped a beat.

Bones gangbangers, two of them. Perfect number. I'd have my hands full taking them out, I knew, but three or more would probably cream me, and just one might not take the hit. They approached. My mind raced to come up with a plan of attack.

The first kid stood a couple inches shorter than the other, but stocky. His buddy, taller and thinner, seemed content to follow. Both loomed over me by several intimidating inches.

I frisked them with my gaze. No guns. I figured blades in the back pockets, though.

Stocky sauntered up and looked at the map. "Well now, let's see what we got."

The other circled behind me and looked at the map from behind, his shoulders level with my ears.

I felt like a trapped rabbit, knowing from training to always avoid getting surrounded. If it came to blows, I'd want them in line, in front. But I gambled that they wouldn't mug someone on their front doorstep. They'd want me in a dark alley somewhere. Right where I wanted them.

I continued my story, laying it on thick.

"My ma said to meet her back at the zoo about an hour ago. She's in town for the convention, you know. But I musta got off at the wrong station, I reckon. That subway shore can be confusin'."

"Nice camera, man," said Lanky from behind me.

"Oh, thanks. Hey, neat ballcaps you guys got."

"Well, gee, kid, thanks." Stocky clapped me on the shoulder. From behind his lips a couple gold capped teeth smiled back.

I held out my hand. "My name's Vern, Vern Bozowski."

Stocky clasped my hand and shook, smiling much longer than needed. "Curly."

I felt his handshake, gauging his strength. Solid and strong. I shook it vigorously, like an overpolite country bumpkin, but didn't give a hint at my full strength. Curly pointed to Stretch.

"This is Rude."

"Well, howdy-do." I turned and shook his hand from over my shoulder. I couldn't gauge his strength very well that way, but I had a good idea. Wiry, not too strong, and probably a bit slow and awkward.

Curly grabbed a pick comb from his pocket and ran it needlessly through his hair. "Well, I'll tell ya Vern, it ain't too far from here." Wrong. It was miles away. "We'd be glad to show you the way. You know, take you there."

I beamed like a found puppy. "Why, that'd be right kind-a y'all."

"Come on. This way." Curly motioned down the street.

My heart sank. It really *was* the way to the zoo. And I would not ruffle these guys unprovoked.

Curly led. Rude fell in beside me as we walked. At the end of the street he turned. The wrong way.

The hair on my neck tingled, and I tensed slightly. I forced the feeling away, saving it for the right moment.

I babbled on. "You know, my friends back home, they all said you New York fellers would be mean and stuff."

"Aw, that ain't true," Curly answered. Rude snickered.

"They shore did. But everyone I've met, they've been great."

The road curved. Curly turned and entered a dark alley. A very, *very* dark alley. I stopped. Rude missed the halt and took an extra half step forward before turning to look back.

"Um, guys, are y'all sure that's the way? It—it looks kinda dark."

Curly shrugged. "Oh, sure. This is a shortcut. Besides, there's these bullies that hang out up the street. Wouldn't wanna run into them. They might mug us."

Rude chuckled and nodded. "Yeah, they might mug us."

"Well, okay. I guess so." I stepped into the darkness, acting just a little hesitant but still trusting, like they would expect from a country bumpkin.

We faded deeper into the shadows.

Curly asked casually over his shoulder, "So tell me. Your ma and pa, what do they do?"

"Oh, well, Pa, he's dead."

"Aww, tough breaks, kid." Jelly oozing out everywhere.

I burned inside with the memories of my real father, axed by a hood just like Curly. And from the same gang. Adrenaline rushed through me full bore, heart chugging like it was about to derail. My muscles tensed, ready for the showdown. I wanted to pound them right then and there, but again training took over. Just a few more seconds to lay the trap.

I continued to spin my yarn. "And me and my ma, well we run the farm. But our real money comes from the oil wells."

That was all the gangsters needed. With a *flick-flick*, their stilettos snapped open. Curly spun and faced me, blade in hand.

Rude flanked me. They prodded me toward the alley wall.

"What the—" I blurted in false surprise. I opened my eyes wide, and backed up without resistance. My left foot bumped a metal garbage can. The rough brick wall scraped against my back.

Calm and self-assured, Curly smiled. "Well, *farm boah*," he began in thick, mocking drawl, "less'n ya wanna see yo' Pa sooner than you'd like, I reckon you'd best be handin' over some of that oil money in yo' pocket." Narrowing his eyes, he finished in his real accent, "The camera and backpack, too, kid."

My mind played out the scenario from a bird's eye view, like I'd learned in training. Rude on left at ten o'clock, blade in right hand; Curly on right at two o'clock, blade in left hand. Each gangster held his weapon at chest level, arms stretched toward me for maximum intimidation. But an extended arm must recoil before it strikes. And that takes time.

I came up with a solution.

With trembling left hand, I pulled the wallet from my hip pocket. I lifted the camera strap from behind my neck with my right hand. I wound the strap around my wrist and gripped tight.

"Pl-please don't hurt me," I whimpered.

I held out the wallet to Rude. Just before he grabbed it, I let go. The billfold fell to the ground. Instinctively, he bent down for it. As he did, I kicked up hard and smashed the bridge of his nose. With a shriek he sprang backwards. His head hit the pavement with a *thud*, out cold.

At the same instant, I backhanded the camera at Curly's head. The metal telephoto lens bounced off his noggin like a pitcher's wild throw. He cried in pain. Swinging the camera full circle, I tried to whip his blade away. I missed, but the camera thwacked into his stomach. He doubled over.

But the street fighter wasn't finished so easily. He looked up, eyes burning in rage. I dropped the camera to the side.

Curly's anger overwhelmed him. Arm fully extended, he aimed the knife squarely at my belly. With a battle cry, he charged.

I pivoted on one foot and stepped back. The blade sailed past. I grabbed his wrist and bicep and pushed hard in the direction of his charge. His momentum carried him on.

Of course, the wall got in his way.

Just as he hit brick, I slammed forward at his arm and wrenched back on his wrist with a crippling Aikido arm bar. He screamed. The knife clattered away.

He rebounded. I turned into him and crouched, my back meeting his stomach. I pulled and lifted. He tumbled over me in a Judo flip, landing square in the scummy trash can.

His butt splattered into the garbage, body wedging tight into the can. I stepped back, breathing rapidly. I gathered the weapons, my wallet and the camera.

Rude slowly came to, moaning and holding his head. He propped up on a wobbly arm. Conscious, but down for the count.

I sat hard on Curly's stomach. Air rushed from his chest with an *"Argh!"*

From this makeshift throne, with Curly as my seat cushion, I kept an eye on both gangbangers.

I began the interrogation. "You know Curly, you guys busted my camera," I said, this time in my normal Brooklyn accent.

"Who are you? What gang you with?" Curly squeaked from below me. I jumped up and back down, knocking another breath from him.

"Yo, Bone*head*, I'm asking the questions here."

"Bonehead?" Curly exclaimed. "You'd better get lost, kid. Our gang's gonna kick your—" I bounced on him again. *"Argh!"*

"Curly, I'm outta here just as soon as you tell me what I want to know. Stall, and we can go all night. Now, tell me about Sly Barett. Where do I find him?" I cleaned my fingernails with Curly's stiletto.

"I don't know any—*argh!* Honest, ain't never heard of no Sly Barett."

"Hmm, good grammar." From my shirt pocket I pulled the newspaper photo of Sly and stuck it in Curly's face. "Okay, how 'bout this guy?"

His eyes widened. His jaw dropped. He recovered and snapped his lips tight, as if the information would slip out on its own.

I tried to settle his anxiety. "I'll tell you this much, Curly. I'm nobody, from nowhere. No gang, no cop, no nothin'. You'll never see me again. Promise."

I put the photo back and resumed picking a nail with the knife, this time inches above his face. He focused on the blade, eyes bulged and crossing like a cartoon. I flicked a piece of dirt away. He flinched.

"What's his name, Curly, and where can I find him?"

"All right, all right. His name's Saul. I—I don't know no last name. He's a gang officer. Hangs out at Buster's Bar a lot, okay? Now get off my—*argh!*"

"Not so fast, gangboy." I knew Buster's would be a neighborhood night club, visited only by locals. Even if I could get in with a fake I.D., I'd stand out like a zit on a nose. "His 'crib', if you guys still call it that. Where? Give me an address."

"Go Google it—*argh!*"

"You think I'd go to this trouble if it was listed? I ain't as dumb as you look, you know."

"We don't know where he—*argh!* Honest, man, we don't. He hangs out at Bones headquarters, down on Brown and 38th. But that's all I know. He comes and goes when he wants."

I sighed. All this risky work for nothing. There had to be something else. I looked back down at Curly.

"How about a girlfriend?"

"None."

"Her name's Mira," Rude said in muffled voice, still doubled over on the pavement.

"Rude," Curly snapped.

"What's the big deal?" Rude said. "Just get rid of the kid."

Curly forced a sigh, which came out as a moan under my weight. He sang.

"All right. Her name's Mira Dominguez. She works at one of the sweatshops Saul runs."

"Which one?"

He pointed down the street. "That abandoned brownstone three blocks over, on Bloomington."

"When?"

"Night shift, I think. They run 24-7 of course, and the graveyard gets off at, like, five a.m. or something."

"You guys aren't lyin', are you?" I asked. "'Cause, I know where you live and stuff. I could always come back. Or I could send others."

Rude replied, "Thought you said you was alone."

"I lied," I lied.

Curly grunted, "No, it's true, man. 'Course, he big with a lot of the babes. But Mira's number one with him right now."

"Good. I believe you." I stood.

I started to walk out of the alley, stepping clear of Rude in case he had any sudden bursts of energy. I turned back and surveyed the battlefield.

I held up a finger. "Ah, guys, I wouldn't' be telling anyone that a single, unarmed little kid creamed you all over the pavement. Might ruin your stellar reputation. Say you tripped and fell down the stairs at the subway or something, like Laurel and Hardy. I won't tell if you won't, okay?" I turned to go, hesitated, and turned back. "Oh, yeah, one more thing. I'm a little short on cash. How bout a loan? Give me your wallets."

"Huh?" they replied in unison.

"Your wallets, guys. Quick, before I get pissed. This really was a pricey camera."

They slowly reached for their billfolds. Rude tossed his to me. Curly pulled out a wallet dripping with fermented garbage.

"Ooh, yuck, Curly. Wipe that off first."

He did, and threw it over. I yanked out the bills, secretly planting a spycam bug deep inside Curly's billfold. I dropped the wallets to the ground.

"Don't know when I can pay you back, so take some advice. Get an honest job, say at a fast food joint. Much safer line of work. Thanks, guys. Later."

"What about our blades, man?" Curly called.

"You should know better than to play with these things, young man. Someone could get hurt."

As I neared the corner of the alley, Curly called one last time.

"Hey, whitey." I looked back. "Nice moves, man."

I nodded, then turned and beat feet, dropping the knives in a dumpster, where they belonged.

CHAPTER 9: FLUSHING PHARAOH

I hid around the block in the shadows of a row-house stoop.

After changing into a black shirt and jeans stashed in my pack, I ditched the nerdy costume in a dumpster.

I pulled out the spyPhone and tuned to the signal from the bug in Rude's wallet. Over the wireless earpiece, I heard him speak. His bashed-in nose sounded like it was pinched with a clothespin.

"I don' know aboud you, but I'm goin' to da hospidal."

Curly replied, "First we gotta report this to the boss."

"Are you jokin'? Like da kid said, who's godda believe a liddle boy kicked our butts?"

"Sooo, we don't tell him that."

They started to move. I followed, keeping far enough back to stay hidden. They made for a local Bones hideout and were quickly ushered in to see their boss.

"What happened to you guys?" a new voice asked.

Curly half cried, "Boss! This gang, this gang of three, uh, *five* huge guys jumped us."

"What gang?"

"Uh, dey didn't have no gang colors, Boss," Rude answered. "But dey had guns and blades. Roughed us up and stole our stileddos. But we gabe 'em a good fight. Curly took two out hisself," he added, trying to boost his leader's image in front of their boss.

"Oh really?" Boss asked skeptically. I imagined him leaning back in his chair and crossing his arms in disbelief.

Curly said, "The leader he—he asked about Saul."

"What? Who was he? What was his name?"

"He said his name was Vern Bozo-sometin'. Uh, big dude. Was askin' for some guy named Sly Barett. But then he showed us a photo of Saul."

"Vern," Boss said slowly. There was a long pause. "Sounds like a cop. Did they have badges?"

"No. No badges, no colors, no nothin'. He—they said they was from out of town."

"What did you tell them?"

"Nothin'. *Nothing*, boss. Honest."

"Yeah right. Get out of my face. But stay close to your cells, I'll be gettin' back to you soon. And you there, go clean yourself up. Looks like you got flattened by a Mack truck."

That was all I could get from the gang. They left, taking my tracker bug with them.

I wandered along the main avenue, gazing at the night crowd. Finally I worked up the nerve to talk to a group of girls standing on a corner. They eyed me like I was a kid cop or something, but finally pointed me to the place.

From the shadows of the alley across the way, I cased the joint. I glanced at my watch. Half past midnight. I yawned. After setting an alarm for 4 am., I curled up under some newspapers in a dark and relatively clean corner of the alley to sleep.

* * *

Through my earpiece, the *beep! beep!* of the spyPhone alarm gently prodded me awake. Yawning, I rubbed my eyes and peered down the alleyway. Twilight was just overtaking the lights of the street. From the field kit in my backpack I pulled out a couple snack bars, water bottle and toothbrush. In five minutes I was full, brushed and ready.

I crept back up the alley. Hiding behind the first set of trash cans, I watched the dilapidated building across the street. A newspaper truck cruised by, its driver tossing a bundle of papers on the curb around the corner.

An hour passed. My eyelids demanded more sleep. My stomach growled in protest. But I was determined to tough it out.

Finally, a cluster of about a dozen women trudged out of the building. They scattered toward their homes, some walking in small groups. Nearly all of them were Asian or Latino. Most of the ladies looked old and withered, like they'd been worked to death for years. Obviously Mira would be Latino, I knew. And she would have to be exceptionally hot for her to catch a gang leader's eye. Hoping for the best, I picked a group of the youngest, prettiest Latinos and followed them.

I hesitated, then called out to the group.

"Mira Dominguez!"

They all stopped and turned around. One spoke up.

"¿*Que*?—what?" she asked. I spied her Hispanic face. Despite her ragged clothes, she had the fresh look of a pretty girl in her late teens.

I knew my half-Japanese light olive skin would make me look to them like a Hispanic as well. So, in my best South American accent, I said in Spanish, "Hello, cousin. I've been looking for you."

She crossed her arms. "Did you call me your cousin?"

"*Si*, it is I, er, Carlos Martinez, your cousin from home."

Her brows shot up in surprise. She laughed. "Can you believe it? My blond, *gringo* cousin from Nicaragua."

The others laughed. I ran my fingers through my dyed hair; I'd forgotten about the disguise.

Her eyes narrowed. "Aren't you a little young to be here in the *Estados Unidos* alone, *compadre*?"

I had to think fast to get her alone without raising suspicion. She said she was from Nicaragua, a place I knew was war-torn and poverty-stricken. My dad had told me that refugees from that place had illegally flooded the States by the thousands.

In Spanish once again, I said, "Your mother sends you greetings, and says to tell you she's coming here to America to live with you."

Putting a slender hand to her lips, she gasped. Beaming, she made a cross with her hand, then pressed them together and said a quick prayer to the sky. The others hooted, and patted her on the back. She said something to them, and they moved on up the street, leaving her alone.

She approached me cautiously. Closer, I could see faint lines crossing her cheeks and telling of a hard, if short, life. Nevertheless, she still looked beautiful.

"What did you say your name was?" she asked.

"Carlos. Take a walk with me, and I'll explain." I turned to go.

She began to follow, but stopped. Her smile faded back to suspicion. "Wait a minute. My mother doesn't even know where I am. They never let me contact her. How could she send *you* to find me?"

I glanced around. "Look, let me level with you. I need your help."

Her eyes widened in anger. "You lie to me about my mother and then ask for my help?" she half screamed.

"Stop," I cried. I held up the wad of cash I'd taken from the gangsters. "Look, here's some money. I'll give you all of it, okay? Just a couple of questions, and I'm gone. But we've got to get off the streets before anyone sees us."

Licking her lips, she eyed the money. Then narrowed her eyes. "Why?"

I held out my arms. "Look at me. I'm a kid. What could I possibly do to hurt you?"

She crossed her arms. "Lure me into a dark alley where your friends are waiting."

"You've grown up on the streets, Mira. You know better than that."

She looked me up and down. "Okay, I'll bite, for a moment. But if you're setting me up, you'll find a switchblade in your gut before you take another step, understand Blondie?"

"*Si.*"

I led her across the street and down the alley where I'd hidden. Just like I had done the night before, she hesitated before stepping into the alley. But by now it was light enough, and the street crowded enough, she knew, to be fairly safe.

"That's far enough," she demanded, stopping halfway.

I turned and said, "Okay. I need your help to find someone."

"Find someone?" she eyed me up and down once again. "Hmm. You're too young to be a cop."

Taking a deep breath, I stepped close to her. She stood taller than me by a couple inches. "I'm searching for my father's killer. You know him as Saul."

She jumped up and backed away, eyes wide. She pointed back down the street. "You'd better go. Go now, boy." She stepped toward the street, but I leaped in front of her.

"Tell me where I can find him, please."

She glared at me. "You want me to narc on my love."

She stepped sideways to get around me. I matched her move. From her back pocket, she flicked out a switchblade. She aimed it toward me like a scolding finger.

"Look, Blondie boy, whoever you are, let me go right now or I cut you up. I will, you know. Like you say, I'm used to the streets."

I called her bluff. Cocking my head sideways, I gazed at her as if bored. With an upturned hand I motioned for her to come. "You don't leave until I have my answer."

She straightened, relaxed and lowered the blade. She leaned on one foot and tapped the other in annoyance. "I can't believe this. Kidnapped by a *kid*. Oh come on, just let me go."

I crossed my arms and slowly shook my head. "No way, señorita Mira."

"I'm warning you. I'll have to—"

She lunged, the blade held at my chest. I grabbed her knife hand at the wrist and twisted, forcing her to the ground. I yanked the knife away and tossed it across the alley. I plopped onto her stomach, legs straddling her waist, and grabbed her wrists.

Her eyes burned up at me in fury. "If you don't let me go this instant, I'll scream."

"Please," I said gently. "Believe me, I'm on your side."

I had to talk fast, before she let out the alarm. Sly was former CIA, and a smuggler, back down in Central America. And she had been smuggled here somehow. I looked deep into her eyes.

Gently I said, "Sly's no friend of yours, Mira Dominguez. He uses you. He smuggled you here from Nicaragua. And in return, you work for him." Her eyes went wide and I could tell I'd guessed right. She swallowed.

"P-please," she begged. "You don't know him. He'll *kill* me. And you."

"Not if I get to him first." I shook her wrists. "Think about it. You came to the States to make it, to leave behind a life of poverty. But what do you have here?" I bent closer. "All alone. Not even your family."

At that, she struggled hard to get free.

"No, no, let me go," she pleaded.

"Yes. Your family. They *all* want to come here, don't they? Leave their poverty behind. And then Sly came along, promising the world. You left with him, hoping to send for your family when you struck it rich.

"But now you're nothing but a slave. Worse than you were before. Cut off from your mother and father. Brothers and sisters." She relaxed her struggle, and looked up at me with tear-filled eyes.

"My big sister insisted that Sly bring me here, too. She did special . . . *favors* for him, to keep us in the sweatshop and not be put out on the street as hookers. But after her accident in the factory, I was left all alone."

Those big, beautiful brown eyes, so sad, struck me deeply, and I relaxed my grip. Instantly she struggled to free herself again.

I pinned her back. "Wait. I can help you. I have . . . connections."

She relaxed again and looked up at me with hope in her eyes. Then she frowned.

"You? A *child*? What 'connections' can you have?"

"Trust me. I *promise* I can help you. But first you've got to help me. Now, I'm going to let you go and we are going to sit here and talk."

She closed her eyes, swallowed, and nodded. I let go and rolled off her. We both sat on the ground, cross-legged, facing each other. I spoke.

"I want to skin your boyfriend alive. But first I need to know more about him."

She held up her hand. "Wait. That *pig* is not my boyfriend. When he brought me here, I was barely a teen. Now that I have grown, I have become his . . . *choice* for the moment, from among his workers. But I get no pleasure from that. It just means I get a few more food scraps and few less beatings every day." She looked up at me, her lips tightening. "I want him dead as much as you do."

"Then you'll help me?"

Her shoulders slumped and she shook her head. "No, Carlos, if that's really your name. I can't. He'll kill me. He'll find out and kill me."

I took a deep breath. "My name's Justin Reed. I'm an orphan. I was trained by the CIA to find my father's killer and his ringleader, the Pharaoh."

"You? A CIA assassin? Hah!"

I scratched my head. "Well, not exactly . . . ."

Her face darkened. She stood, angrily dusting herself off. "You're *muy loco*—very crazy, Justin Reed. Enough of your schoolboy fantasies. Go back to your playground and—"

I jumped up. "Mira, wait! My guardian father is a bigwig in the CIA. He's very powerful. He can get your entire family here—legally. No questions asked." I prayed it was true.

She rolled her eyes. "Oh, *sure*," she said skeptically, but with less conviction this time. A glimmer of hope found its way into those dark browns.

"Look, do you know who the Pharaoh is?"

She shook her head. "No. But I believe I've heard that name before. I've never seen him though. I think Saul meets with him once in awhile."

I grabbed her shoulders. "Listen. A while back Sly worked for the Central Intelligence Agency. That's how he got you here. But then he got busted and sent to jail. A bad guy, a mole in the CIA named the Pharaoh, helped Sly escape in exchange for assassinating my father."

From my backpack I pulled out a spycam bug and held it up. "I can't get near Sly. He might recognize me. But if you can plant this on him, I can find out everything I need."

She took the bug in her hand and examined it. "What? A coat button?"

"It's a spycam." I explained how it worked.

"What should I do with it?"

"Plant it in his wallet, if you can. That way he keeps it on him all the time."

"Is that all?"

"No. Tell him I came looking for him. A boy with long black hair. Not short and blond, like mine is now. Tell him my name is Justin, and I was looking for the key to *Rubber Soul*."

She wrinkled her brows. "The key to what?"

I repeated myself. She looked down at the button, confused.

I wrote down the address of my hotel. "If you have any problems, you can find me here. Thanks for your time." I held up the wad of bills.

She eyed the money, hesitated, then grabbed it. "He's picking me up at two, after I get a few hours' sleep. I'll try to plant it then." She told me the address of the tiny apartment she shared with several coworkers. Then she smiled, both shy and mischievous at the same time. "No fair spying on me before that, okay CIA boy?"

I smiled back. "Okay. And don't worry. I'll find you."

She ruffled my hair. "You're a good kid."

"And you're a good girl, Mira. And I hope we can give you a major career change soon." Blushing, I added, "You're too beautiful to be wasted this way."

She turned at the end of the alley and blew me a kiss. A kiss that made me tremble.

I hoofed it back to the fleabag to catch a few hours' sleep on a real, if rancid, mattress, then caught a train back to Mira's neighborhood. I took the CIA gear plus my skateboard. To keep a low profile, I wore a Yankees ballcap and sunglasses.

Once off the subway and on ground level, I tuned to the frequency for her spycam bug. The signal blared strong in my earphones. I closed in. From a block away, I spotted the apartment building, just the way she'd described it. I backed off. To kill time and avoid suspicion, I skated around the basketball court of a park a half block down.

After a few minutes, a white Cadillac pulled up to her. Through my spyPhone I heard a man's voice.

"Get in, baby." The deep baritone of his words made the hair on my neck bristle. From the CIA video files, I recognized the voice at once. Sly Barett.

Racing out of the chained courtyard, I flagged down a passing cab. As I jumped in, the driver looked around.

"Where to?" he asked with an East Indian accent. I fought off the temptation to say the old line, "Follow that car." But he didn't need to know we were following anyone.

"Just move out," I said frantically. "I'll tell you as we go." He eyed me funny. I threw him a twenty. "Don't ask questions, just move." He shrugged and pulled out.

Over my earpiece, Sly spoke.

"You lookin' good, baby."

"Oh, Saul, it's so good to see you. Listen, you've been so good to me, let me take you out today, okay?" I heard the rustle of money.

"Where'd you get that dough?" Sly exclaimed.

"I've been saving up some money from work."

"What? Give me that."

"But baby, that's mine."

"Well, what's yours is mine, woman," he sneered sarcastically. "Let go of it."

"Well, here then. Let me put it in your wallet for you."

"Hah," I exclaimed.

"What?" the cabbie asked.

"Nothin'." What a great ploy to get into his wallet, I thought.

On the spyPhone screen, I briefly caught a glimpse of Sly through her fingers. I was shocked. His face had completely changed. Plastic surgery, I realized. No wonder he'd evaded the cops all this time. But between his voice and those piercing brown eyes, I still recognized the scumbag. I felt my cheeks flush red with anger and not a little fear. But then the screen went dark again in her hand.

The tracker signal swung.

I jabbed a finger ahead. "Turn right at the light."

The cabbie swerved into the turn lane. A car behind us honked.

Mira continued. "Hey, honey, can't I keep some of that money? I need to go shopping. Here, give me your wallet. I'll just take a twenty."

I heard him slap her hands away. "Get your paws off my bread and shut up."

I followed them all the way to his apartment. She never got the bug planted, I could tell.

I pointed ahead. "Pull over."

The cabbie stopped and I jumped out. He sped off, anxious to get out of the ghetto. Slipping down the nearest alley, I hid behind some trash cans and listened to their conversation.

As they walked into the room she said, "Someone came looking for you this morning."

"Who?"

"Blon-uh, long black haired gringo kid named Justin. Said he was looking for someone named Sly Barett."

"Why didn't you tell me this earlier, woman."

"Because he was just a kid. And he was acting weird, saying strange things. I thought he was just tripping on junk. Kept rambling about a key to *Rubber Soul* or something."

"*What?*" I imagined Sly jumping to his feet in surprise. "Get to the bedroom, *now*," he bellowed. As she left, she somehow planted the spycam on a wall or something, because suddenly Sly's ugly mug came into view on my spyPhone screen. Quickly I snapped a freeze frame of his face for the CIA database.

Pacing the room, Sly put his own cell to his ear. After a brief pause, he spoke. "Pharaoh, this is Saul."

I sucked in my breath.

"Some kid was around this morning asking for me by my old name. And he was askin' about *Rubber Soul*, too. What? Oh, his name was Justin."

Sly paused, then said, "I don't know what he looks like. I didn't see him. Black-haired kid, that's all I know. One of my women met him.

"And another thing. A gang came down here last night and roughed up two of my men real good. They was asking for me by my old name, too." Another pause. "Yes, I think you should get up here right away. First flight. Maybe you can get more out of my men. I'll round them up for you. Shall I pick you up at the airport, sir? No? Okay, I understand. Tonight at eight, then. I'll be here. We'll *all* be here." He hung up.

I shook my fists above my head and mouthed a triumphant *Yes!*

"Mira," Sly shouted, storming past my screen and out of view. But I could still hear his angry voice.

"Hmm?"

"Tonight you ain't workin'. Tonight you meet an old friend of mine. And you tell him everything."

"Of course, Saul."

I heard a hand slap a face. Mira shrieked. "You hear me, woman? *Everything.* Or you're dog meat, you unnastand? Till then, you stay put."

I heard the back door slam shut, then lock. Then footsteps across the floor. Sly came back in view, then left through the front door. I heard it lock.

I clenched my fists. I wanted so badly to run over and set Mira free, or at least talk to her, soothe her fears and coach her on what to say. But I couldn't risk it in broad daylight.

I bolted from my hiding place and skated away.

I took the Five train south and impatiently killed time by skating around Central Park. I tried to freestyle a bit, working the kinks out of my rusty kickflips. But I couldn't concentrate. I was too nervous about the upcoming meeting with Pharaoh.

Worse, it kept feeling like I was being watched. But, the only one that seemed to be paying any attention to me was was some old Asian lady in dark glasses feeding pigeons.

Night fell.

To prepare for the stakeout, I grabbed a couple of burgers and a soda to-go. I ducked into the shadows of the alley facing Sly's place and pulled the CIA gear from my pack. I wrapped the mini binoculars over my neck, stuck in the spyPhone earpiece, then leaned against a trash can and sipped on the soda.

Sly returned, Curly and Rude in tow.

Eight o'clock came. And went. I worried that Pharaoh might not show up, or that he might have taken a back way. Or maybe even be spying on *me*. Suddenly freaked out, I looked all around. With the binocs, I frantically scanned my surroundings, down the dark alley and up on the roofs, switching back and forth between night vision and infra red. Nothing. But then, far down the street, the faint glow of body heat. The dot of red grew to the figure of a man. Swiftly, he approached.

Switching to regular mode, I trained the binoculars on him. My hands trembled, blurring my view.

Obscured in shadow at first, with hat pulled tight, his face I couldn't make. But something about his outline, and his gait, sparked a flicker of recognition inside me. A black trench coat flowed like Darth Vader's cape about his body. He passed beneath a street light and I caught the flash of teeth. Behind a grimace. A wizard's grimace. A bolt of fear blasted up my spine.

"Hoffman," I whispered in shock.

Max Hoffman, Bob's boss and Cole's right hand man. With the binocs, I switched to night vision and scanned the streets for Bob or Cole. But as far I could tell, he was alone.

Hoffman bounded up the stoop and entered the building.

Dropping the field glasses to my chest, I leaned against the alley wall. I began to shake. I rubbed a hand over my face, suddenly wet with sweat. "Calm yourself Justin," I whispered. Closing my eyes, I sucked in a deep breath and held it, like I'd learned in training, forcing the heart to slow. Exhaling, I shook my head.

So, my fake death had been useless. Hoffman was one of only two people in the world who knew I was still alive.

I pulled out the spyPhone, and with a finger held the earpiece in tight. Watching the screen, I punched the Video Record button to capture the whole scene.

On a zebra striped sofa against the far wall, Curly and Rude sat fidgeting nervously beneath a huge, butt-ugly abstract painting. Mira sat, still and quiet, in a corner chair. All eyes were on Sly as he paced the room before them. Sly turned as he heard Hoffman's footsteps tromping up the rickety stairs. Everyone jumped as Hoffman pounded twice on the door. When Sly cracked it open, the Pharaoh bounded in, knocking him backward.

Recovering, Sly said, "He-hello, sir. Everyone, I want you to meet—"

"Never mind my name. 'Sir' will do," Hoffman/ Pharaoh growled.

"Yes, sir," he squeaked, cowering away. Even Sly, the hardened killer, was scared to death of the man.

Hoffman immediately grilled Mira. I knew his cunning interrogation tricks, and prayed she wouldn't slip up. Hoffman went over her story three times, from every angle, trying to trip her up on the details. But he never did. He asked her one last question that made me raise a brow.

"Mira, does Justin know of my plan?"

"What plan? I don't know anything, I tell you."

"Forget it." Hoffman turned to Curly. "So, another gang took you out, hmm?"

"Yes, sir. Four of them."

"I thought it was five."

Slight pause. "Oh, yeah. That's what I meant to say. Uh, five."

"Then why are you still alive?"

Another pause as Curly glanced at Rude. "Well, when they saw that we wouldn't talk, they—"

"*Bull*. Describe them. Each one. In detail."

"The leader's name was Vern Bozo-something," Sly interjected.

"What?" Hoffman exclaimed. "Vern Bozowski?"

Curly nodded. "Yeah, that's him. That's the guy. Uhh . . . big guy. Huge guy."

Crossing his arms, Hoffman loomed over the gangster. "Oh, really? Go on."

I couldn't help but snicker as Curly stammered through a weak description of a couple make-believe hoods. But his limited imagination soon ran out.

From inside his coat, Hoffman slowly drew out his H&K pistol, silencer attached. I gulped. Cocking it, he held it to Curly's head. "Lie to me one more time, boy, and your brains will be part of that butt-ugly painting behind you. Understand?"

"Y-yes sir."

"Now. One more time. There weren't five big guys, were there? There was just one. A kid. Correct?"

"*What*," Sly exclaimed. "There's no way my men could be taken out by—"

"Shut up till you're spoken to."

"I'm sorry, sir," Sly blubbered.

"Just one kid, right? A single, solitary, scrawny little kid."

Curly let out a breath. "Yeah."

"So, Curly, he robbed you, but left your wallets, hmm?"

"Yes, sir."

"Your wallets. Give them to me."

There was no protest from the gang. I switched frequencies to the bug hidden in Rude's wallet, and immediately heard a loud swishing noise.

"You idiots!" Hoffman screamed. Suddenly the Pharaoh's face, eyes and veins bulging, filled the screen. His voice blasted through my eardrums. "Justin, if you can hear me, you're *dead*!"

Instinctively I jerked back, as if he could climb through the screen and squash me right there. He threw the mini cam to the floor. I heard a grinding noise as Hoffman smashed it with his boot.

I switched back to Mira's bug and listened.

"Mira, give me your purse," he demanded.

I gulped. If he found Mira's bug, she was sunk. And so was I.

He rifled through the bag, then dumped its contents on the wooden floor. Everything rattled out.

"Hmm, nothing," he mumbled. He seemed to be satisfied with that. I swiped a hand across my forehead. "Wait, what's this?" My heart skipped a beat. Hoffman read aloud the address to my hotel. He'd found my message.

Mira tried to act casual. "Oh, that? Some drunk gave me his address and told me to meet him for a drink. I took it just to get rid of him."

"Don't lie to me," Hoffman said quietly. He backhanded her, hard. She shrieked. He hit her again, sending her to the floor. As she raised up on an arm, blood trickled from the side of her mouth. I clenched my hands and teeth in rage. What could I do? Four of them against me, and Hoffman, a trained killer, armed. I watched helplessly.

Mira pleaded with him, sobbing. "It's nobody, I *swear*."

Hoffman ignored her. To Sly he barked, "If the Dodger was eavesdropping on us, he can't hear us now. He's running back to his hotel room to grab his gear and escape. Cut him off. Your boys will get the revenge they crave. And after they've worked him over, I want you to bring him back here alive. Above all, *alive*. Break every bone in his body if you wish, but if he's killed, every one of you will die a slow and painful death. Do you hear me? I *must* interrogate him." They all nodded vigorously, eyes wide.

"You're not coming, sir?" Sly asked.

"No. I have to get back to Washington. I have to be seen at a funeral tomorrow afternoon. People will expect me there. I'll return tomorrow night."

Sly pointed at Mira. "What about her?"

"Lock her up in the interrogation room. After you catch Justin, soften her up for me. I'll deal with her when I get back."

"No," she screamed, tears streaming from her eyes. "I know nothing, I swear." Her voice faded as Sly and the boys dragged her past the spycam.

Everyone left, leaving Mira alone. I sank deep into the shadows and watched the four criminals pile in to Sly's Cadillac and peel out. Once they turned the corner, I sprinted to the apartment and bounded up the stairs, the tracker directing me to the right door.

I bent to the doorknob, pulled out the Swiss Army picks and went to work. It was a typical pin cylinder lock and easy to pick. I stuck the torsion wrench in the bottom of the keyhole and twisted lightly. With my other hand I inserted the feeler pick and slowly raised each tumbler into place. In less than a minute, the door popped open.

I ran down the hall. "Mira," I shouted.

"In here!"

Her muffled voice came from behind a solid steel security door. My heart sunk. "Mira, its locked with a key," I said.

"Saul does that so he can punish his workers."

"He does more than that in there, I'll bet," I answered. "Give me a minute."

"Get out of here, Justin. You can't help me."

I knelt down to the lock. This one was a pro job. Even with my CIA training, I wasn't sure I could do it. I set to work. Worried about tripping a silent alarm, I kept glancing over my shoulder for the gang's return. It took five excruciating minutes of sweating, glancing and prodding, but finally the last tumbler gave way. I opened the door to Mira's gaping mouth.

"How did you—"

"Grab your stuff, Mira, quick. If there's any cash in the apartment, take it." I grabbed her by the shoulders. "Mira, do you know what Hoffman meant by his plan?"

She shook her head. "No. But I know that he plans things with Saul. In there." She pointed to the rear bedroom. I raced up to the door and tried it. Locked, by two more standard tumblers. I bent to them, and in a few minutes popped both locks. We crept inside.

Sunlight penetrated the blue curtains and lit the room in an eerie glow. I spied a map of the world tacked to the wall. Colored pins skewered several countries, with lines of thread streaming from point to point. I leaned closer and studied the layout. Lines led from Arizona to Baja California, from South to North America; several others weaved through the Mideast, Asia, North Africa and Europe. Nearly every corner of the globe.

"His smuggling routes," I said.

I wondered why Pharaoh didn't have his network encrypted on a database somewhere, instead of a simple paper chart system older than Magellan. Then I realized, no one could hack a paper map.

I studied the plan. Far more pins dotted the world than could account for drug routes, or even spy networks. Gold pins stuck in Washington, Moscow, Beijing, London . . . .

"What's he planning?" I thought aloud.

It had to be something big, something that tied the governments of the world into his plan.

After snapping some shots of the board with my spyPhone, I pulled Mira out and down the stairs, then peeked out the front door. All clear, as far as I could tell. I brandished my skate like a broadsword, ready to swing. We snuck out and caught a cab.

"Where are we going?" Mira asked as we hopped in.

"Brooklyn."

CHAPTER 10: FUNERAL FOR A CLOSE FRIEND

We checked into a hotel around the corner from my old orphanage. Stains smeared the peeling wallpaper of the room, but compared to the fleabag I'd stayed at in the Bronx, it was the Ritz.

Once safely in the room and out of earshot of curious cabbies and nosey neighbors, Mira asked, "So, now that you've ruined my life, what's our plan?"

I stretched my tired muscles, then pulled the bedspread off the mattress. "You get the bed, I get the floor. That's our plan."

She eyed me. "You've got to come up with a better one than that."

"Look, I've got to get up early tomorrow. I want you to stay here for a few days, okay?"

Fists on hips, she stood and faced me. "You ruin my life, almost get me killed, and now you want me to just *hang around*?"

"Yes. You've got to lay low while I take care of our . . . mutual problem. When I'm done, you'll see why."

She sighed, blowing a lock of hair straight up from over her gorgeous eyes. "I have a friend who lives near here. I could—"

I held up a hand. "No friends. That's the first place they'll check."

"Guess so." She raised her head high. "But I am *not* staying here."

I sighed. "We'll argue about it in the morning." I lay down on the ground and wrapped the bedspread around me.

Another thought struck me. I looked up at her. "Mira, is there anything else you do for Sly? Any other kind of work, I mean?"

She shook her head. "Not really. Sometimes he'll fix me and some of the other girls up as kind of escorts at his business parties."

I raised my brows. "Fix you up with whom?"

"His business contacts. The ones we sell our goods to, I guess."

"From?"

She scrunched her face, as if unsure. "Oh, I don't know, all kinds of places. Europe, Saudi Arabia, South America. Lots of Chinese."

"And you just, um, socialize with them? Nothing else?"

Crossing her arms, she squared her jaw. "No hanky panky, if that's what you're thinking. We may be his slaves in a way, but we *do* have our dignity."

"Glad to hear it. But, no, what I meant was, he doesn't have you, um, pass on any kind of messages to them?"

"Well, we always have a special envelope to give them. A letter of some kind."

I bit my lip. "Have you ever read the letter?"

She shook her head vigorously. "No way. Strict orders not to open them. They're sealed tight. I'm sure it's just a boring letter of thanks for their business, anyway. Sometimes the customer will have a letter for Sly, too. Why?"

"Nothing."

But I knew exactly what those letters contained. Sly used Mira and her girlfriends as unwitting couriers to smuggle government secrets to foreign spies. Secrets Hoffman had stolen.

I turned off the light. We lay there in darkness for a while, chatting like kids at a camp out.

"You seem to know a lot about me," she said.

"A few lucky guesses."

"Well, you were right about Saul, or Sly, as you call him. When he met my family in El Salvador, he said he was this big fashion agent from New York, scouting for fresh talent. Said he'd take my sister back to the States and make her a high fashion model. But when we got here, he turned into an animal. He beat my sister, kept us locked up. Told me if we disobeyed him, he would turn us in to Immigration. We knew nothing about your police, and feared they'd be worse than him. It was a nightmare." She shook her head in disbelief. "We were stupid, naive. We should've known better. It was all our fault."

"No, don't say that. He lied to you. Used you like a slave."

She spoke softly, half to herself, her confession spilling out as if bottled up for years. "I work 18 hours a day for him, pretend to like him, and get nothing more than a room and a beating out of it.

"I look into the eyes of each man that passes me by on the street, hoping a knight in shining armor will come and sweep me away from all this. But they never do." She sighed deeply, rolled over and looked down at me. "Thank you. Whatever comes of it, I am glad it's over. Even if it means deportation. Or my life."

"Neither will happen. I promise."

"Hmph, I wish I could believe you, Sir Lancelot. Or should I say, Sir Dodger?"

With my head I gave a dramatic, mocking bow. "Call me Justin, milady."

She giggled. "Okay, Sir Justin."

* * *

I got up before dawn, took a quick shower and dressed. I slapped on the ballcap and stuffed my board and CIA gear into Carlos's duffel.

Mira still slept. I tiptoed to the bed and by the dim lamplight gazed down at her. Her cheeks glowed with life, lips parted in a peaceful smile. The harsh lines of her life as a sweatshop slave already seemed to be fading away. I nudged her. She stirred. She opened her eyes and looked deeply into mine. My pulse kicked up a gear.

"I gotta go," I said. "If I'm not back in twelve hours, go straight to the cops. Don't open the door for anyone but me. I'll call you when I can. If the phone rings, pick it up and listen, but don't say anything till you hear my voice."

"Wow, you sound like you've been on the run all your life."

"I have, in a way."

She grabbed me, pulled me down and kissed me. I pulled back and blinked. And—I can't believe it—I blushed.

"What was that for?"

"Because you slept in the same room without taking advantage of me. No one's done that in a long time."

I thumped my chest. "Sir Justin must stay chivalrous for his fair maiden while he slays the evil dragon."

She giggled. "You're certainly that, Sir Justin. But you forgot one detail. I'm going with you."

I opened my mouth to argue, then sighed. "Do you know how to drive?"

"*Si.*"

"Okay, come on. But hurry up, there's not much time."

She showered and dressed in record time. Once outside, I pulled my ballcap tight and slipped on a pair of shades. We strolled around the corner, arm in arm like boyfriend/girlfriend. When we got to a point opposite the main entrance to the orphanage, I stopped. I glanced left and right, then pulled her into the recessed doorway of an apartment building. Her body blocked others from seeing me.

Her face lay inches from mine, her sweet breath puffing gently on my cheeks. My pulse raced. I blushed again, and hoped she couldn't see it in the pale light of the New York overcast.

She smiled a sly smile. "Getting fresh all of a sudden, Sir knight?"

"Sorry, no. Um, necessary for cover."

"Un huh," she said teasingly. "So, what are we doing here?"

"Waiting for a bus."

"Oh, yeah? Doesn't look like a bus stop. Where are we going?"

"To a funeral."

"Oh? Who died?"

"Me."

She pulled away and eyed me. While we waited, I explained the whole story of my code name Dodger, of Operation *Rubber Soul*, and the plan I had in mind.

Hoffman had said he was going to a funeral. My funeral, I knew. He had to be seen there to avoid suspicion. Bob would be there, too. And I knew the orphanage would bus my friends down to Washington for it, too. I figured we'd hitch a ride.

Sure enough, after awhile an old yellow school bus pulled up.

"Come on." I pulled her by the arm across the street. As the driver opened the bus door, we bounded in. Old and slow, he didn't have time to block the way.

"Hey kids, we're not ready to go yet," he protested.

I plopped our bags in a seat. As I did, I pulled out the bottle of chloroform from my CIA kit. I doused a rag with the knockout liquid and held it behind my back.

Approaching him I said, "Oh, gee, I'm sorry." I pointed out the window. "Hey, what's that?" As he turned to look, I slapped the rag over his mouth. He slumped in the seat. I swung the bus doors shut and Mira helped me drag him to the back.

"He'll be out for awhile. Here, Mira, help me get the emperor out of his clothes."

She swiftly unbuttoned his uniform coat and shirt and yanked them off.

I smirked. "Wow, you're a pro at that."

Wrinkling her nose, she punched my arm. "Watch it, Blondie, or I'll teach you some other survival skills I've learned."

I slipped the driver's baggy uniform over me, then put on the cap. The huge thing fell down over my eyes. I made a goofy face.

"How do I look?"

Mira laughed. "Eat about a hundred donuts, and you'll be fine."

I led her to the front and showed her how to drive the bus, pointing out the gears and levers.

She looked up. "How in the world do you know how to drive a school bus?"

"I learned the hard way, when Randy and I escaped from the orphanage last Spring."

A cop car pulled up in front of us. I sucked in my breath.

"Duck," I whispered.

We hid behind the front seats. I peeked out at the action. The officer got out and opened the back door of his car. A figure in handcuffs climbed out. I recognized the prisoner.

"Speak of the devil, it's him."

"Who?"

"Randy. The one who stole the bus with me."

"Looks like history is about to repeat itself."

"Yeah. Hope it doesn't turn out the same way."

The policeman escorted him to the front door of the orphanage. He released the cuffs and led him inside. After a minute, the cop came out and drove off. Alone.

My friends filed out the front door. All trudged along listlessly, heads hanging low. Randy and Doug led, talking in low tones. Sherry and a few others from our floor followed, all sniffling.

I jerked my head toward the back. "Okay, Mira, hide for a minute."

She ducked behind a seat in back as I sat in the driver's chair. I slipped on my shades and pulled up my collar. I pushed the lever and opened the doors.

As they climbed in, I turned the other way, peering sideways in the mirror as they reached the back. Mira sat up. The kids looked at her funny, then Sherry gasped as she spotted the naked bus driver, passed out and lying in a seat. Mira held a finger to her lips and smiled mischievously. They seemed to get the idea, and sat down as if nothing was wrong.

Once they were all on, I reached for the lever to close the doors.

Then Mrs. Kraumas waddled up.

I'm sunk, I thought. It hadn't crossed my mind that the Kraut might go.

She clambered aboard. Waving a paper in my face, she said between wheezes, "Here you go, sir. The directions to the cemetery."

I sank deeper into the coat collar and grumbled in my lowest tone. After grabbing the note I turned away, pretending to read.

Kraut said, "I'm so sorry I can't make it. I *really* wanted to go. Justin was *such* an angel. But I'm afraid there's been an emergency here and—well, a matron's work is never done. Please drive safely." She turned to go, sniffling as she stepped down. "Oh, here come the tears again. I'm so upset, he was such a lovely child." She stepped off the bus, then turned back. "Randy's on 24-hour emergency leave from the juvenile correctional center. Somehow that nice psychiatrist Dr. Cheney arranged it, though for the life of me I've never heard of such a thing."

"Mmmhmm," I mumbled gruffly.

She leaned her head back in and, with a conspiratorial whisper, added, "I think he shouldn't be any trouble today. Justin *was* Randy's best friend." Sniffling, she turned away. "Oh, I'm so upset. It's all so *horrible* . . . ." Her voice faded as she waddled off.

I shut the bus doors. Nearly bursting with joy, I stood, turned and removed the cap and sunglasses. I grinned the biggest grin ever.

I shouted, "Where to, kids?"

"Ju-Justin?" Randy squeaked. Tearing up, I opened my arms wide.

"In the living flesh!"

The bus erupted in cheers. Everyone crowded forward and hugged me.

Wiping his tears away, Randy asked, "What gives, you lunatic?"

"And where'd you get that dorky blond hair?" Doug chimed in.

"First, let me introduce my partner in crime, Mira." I held a palm toward her. With a smile and wave, she took the driver's seat and started up. We drove off.

My friends crowded around. Over the bus's PA system, I told them some of the story—on a need-to-know basis, of course—and the plan I had for them. By the time we made Washington, everyone knew their part.

Mira, now wearing the driver's cap, uniform and sunglasses, pulled into the cemetery where my empty coffin would be buried. I spotted a parking space far enough away to keep hidden while I watched with the binoculars. I bent over Mira's shoulder and pointed.

"There." She parked.

The slate gray overcast wept rain. A perfect setting for saying goodbye to Justin Malcomb Reed, I thought with a smile.

Bob, Cole and Hoffman all pulled up at the same time, all driving separate cars. They strolled across the lawn and stood solemnly by the grave. I lifted the binoculars, and spied the spies.

Tears filled Bob's eyes; he sniffled. An academy award performance if he was guilty, I thought.

But that was my gamble. Dad was innocent, I knew. My gut told me Bob wore the white hat, too. If not, I really would be buried soon.

Others gathered about the grave, including Glen Keller. Tears streamed down his cheeks. Beside him cried his sister Joya, the tough but gorgeous blonde tomboy whom I hardly knew. My own eyes filled at the sight. I searched for Carlos, but he never showed. I frowned, disappointed. Even though he knew I was alive, I figured he'd show up so the others wouldn't suspect.

I dropped the field glasses to my chest. "Doug, give me your back," I said. He bent over and I used him as a table to scribble a note on a piece of paper. I couldn't resist starting the message with a quote from Mark Twain, another of my favorite authors:

> Fagin,
> The reports of my death are greatly exaggerated.
> Hoffman is Pharaoh! I've got proof. I don't know if Cole is in on it.
> Meet me at the ugly green Bermuda shorts.
> Dodger

I handed Doug the note, which he palmed.

"Where's my bug?" Randy asked. I handed him the coat button cam.

"Put this in your pocket so I can listen to the funeral," I explained. "It's too big to plant on Hoffman, though. He'd spot it. So use this on him instead. I held up the black pebble tracker. Hold this in your fingers, and when you get the chance, squish it into his coat. It'll squirt out glue and stick to the cloth."

Through the field glasses, I pointed out their targets.

Before opening the doors, I announced, "Okay everyone, remember your parts. Long faces like you had at the orphanage. I'm dead, remember? Break a leg."

The kids filed off the bus. Doug snickered, breaking his character.

Randy elbowed him. "Shut up, you idiot. Act the part."

When the last one stepped off, I closed the doors, tuned into the spyPhone and watched with Mira from the back of the bus.

I crossed my fingers. "If anyone messes up, the whole plan will be blown."

"Don't worry, Justin," Mira said with a smirk. "All your friends seem to be born con artists."

I groaned. "Thanks a lot."

As the funeral began, Sherry cracked up. I held my breath and trained the binocs on her. Everyone turned and looked at her. She squinted and crinkled her nose, buried her face in her hands, and turned the laugh into a cry. Everyone seemed to buy it. I sighed in relief.

The minister preached on.

"I am told that our beloved Justin was fond of the story *Oliver Twist*, so I would like to quote an appropriate passage. 'We need to be careful how we deal with those about us, when every death carries to some small circle of survivors, thoughts of so much omitted, and so little done—of so many things forgotten, and so many more which might have been repaired! There is no remorse so deep as that which is unavailing.'"

Randy started his act. He sneered. "Remorse. Yeah, right."

Doug elbowed him. "Knock it off." The others glared.

Randy said, "You knock it off. I got no remorse. Justin kept his fat trap shut while I took the rap for him. I hated his guts. I just came here to get out of Juvy for a day."

Doug lunged at him. The boys toppled to the ground, swinging. Sherry screamed—her part in the act. A couple orphans pulled them away, but they jumped each other again. Doug tackled Randy and knocked him straight into Hoffman, who fell backward into a thick puddle of mud. Randy flopped on top of him.

I threw my head back, laughed aloud and clapped.

"Bravo," I cheered.

"*Olé,*" Mira added with a fist in the air.

I couldn't see Randy plant the tracker, but I knew he would. With all eyes on Hoffman and Randy wallowing in the mud, Doug stuffed the note in Bob's hand. The ever perfect field spy, he covered his surprise and slipped the note in his pocket.

Hoffman stood and, growling, slapped at his filthy raincoat.

Bob made the two boys apologize to each other, then all stood quiet for the rest of the ceremony. After the service, the kids boarded the bus. Grinning wide, Randy and Doug marched down the aisle. I slapped their backs.

"Perfect show, guys. Oscar performances!"

"Bob took the message like he expected it," Doug said.

"I saw. Randy, great move on Hoffman. He got what he deserved. Did you plant the bug?"

"Yep. Inside his raincoat. But I hope your little gizmo works in the mud."

I laughed. "Just fine."

"Oh, and I got this for you. I knew you was low on cash, so I took the liberty." Randy held out a wallet.

My eyes went wide. *Hoffman's?* He nodded. "Geez, Randy, you just picked the pocket of the most dangerous man on the planet." But, as I stuffed Hoffman's billfold in my pocket, I couldn't help but laugh. "Thanks, you moron."

"Now what?" Doug asked.

"Mira takes you guys back home. Whenever the driver comes to, slap him with another rag of chloroform for a few seconds. When you get back, just leave him there with his clothes. He won't say anything, 'cause he won't know what happened."

I took Sherry by the hand. "I'll be back in a couple days. Think you can sneak Mira into the orphanage and hole her up till then?"

She nodded. "No problem, Dodgerboy."

We drove off. I directed Mira to the mall for my secret meeting with Bob. We pulled up to a side entrance. I said goodbye.

I shook Randy's hand. "I owe you again. When this is over I'm going to pay you back. Big time. I promise."

"Don't mention it."

"It's gotta be miserable in there. I don't know how you can take it."

"Hey, I'm a survivor. Besides, I'm learning lots more dirty tricks in Juvy than I ever could back at the orphanage."

Punching him on the shoulder, I chuckled and nodded. I turned to Doug. "Take care of the girls, as I know only you can."

"With pleasure, master," he said with a low bow.

When I got to Mira, she scooped me in her arms and smacked a huge kiss on my lips that practically knocked me out. The others hooted.

Sherry stomped up the aisle. She sneered at Mira in jest. "Wait a minute. He's still mine you, you home breaker." To another round of cat calls, Sherry planted one on me that equaled her rival's.

Nearly dizzy, I pulled out my backpack and board, stepped off the bus and waved.

I ran to the store where we'd seen the ugly green Bermuda shorts. No Bob.

Suddenly, I had the creepy feeling of being watched. I searched all around but saw no one. Chills buzzed down my spine as I remembered the attempted hit at the mall in New York.

From the backpack I pulled out the spyPhone and tuned to Hoffman's signal. The range read 1,500 feet. I gasped. Way too close. I mixed in with the shopping crowd. Punching the spyPhone Audio Record button, I reluctantly crept towards Pharaoh's signal. I *had* to spot him first, or I was dead meat.

At a mall exit I spied a commotion outside. There, in the parking lot, next to his parked Vette, stood Bob—surrounded by Pharaoh's henchmen. They grabbed Bob and brutally shoved him into Hoffman's Mercedes. The kidnappers sped off.

"No," I screamed. I sprinted outside, forgetting myself.

But they were gone.

I had to call King Cole. I still didn't know if he was in on it, but now I had no choice. But Cole and Hoffman had taken my emergency contact earpiece, and my stolen spyPhone was totally offline. I sprinted to Bob's Vette, hoping to grab his cell. I peered inside. His phone still sat in its hands-free charging cradle. Kneeling by the driver's door, I quickly picked the lock. The car alarm blasted my eardrums. I climbed in, shut the siren off and reached for the phone.

Something hard and cold pressed against the back of my head. The muzzle of a pistol. I froze.

"Don't bother with the phone, boy," a voice boomed from the back seat. The hair on my neck bristled at the deep baritone voice of Sly Barett.

CHAPTER 11: PHARAOH'S LAIR

Through the rear view mirror, I saw him. Sly's dark brown eyes shined, as if he got off on holding guns to kids' heads. I recognized his pistol from weapons training. An Austrian Glock 19, with seventeen deadly rounds of ammo.

He shed the lap blanket he'd hidden under and slithered into the front seat. With his free hand he pulled out Bob's key and fired up the Vette.

I scowled. "What do you want from me, you scumbag?"

He jabbed the pistol in my side. "No yacking, boy. Just start drivin'."

"Um, I'm only a kid. I, I don't know how to—"

"I know about your training. Shut up and drive," he demanded.

Sly waved me out of the parking lot and down a side street. With his free hand he reached up and pulled out Bob's cell from its charge cradle. He dialed, then held the phone to his ear. His eyes never left me.

He said into the receiver, "Sly here. I got the kid. We'll be at the warehouse in twenty minutes. Right." He fumbled with the phone, trying to hang it up.

I reached for it. "Oh, here, I can do it." He tensed, but then relaxed and let me take the receiver. "It's a bit tricky, you see. It slides into the charger like this."

As I clicked the phone into the cradle, I secretly reached around and punched the memory button that dialed Cole's office. At least, I hoped that was the one I'd pushed.

After a moment, I started talking. I was tempted to tell him off, say what a scumbag he was for killing my father. But instead I tried to steal as much information from him as I could.

"So, Sly, what warehouse are we going to? If I knew, I could get us there quicker."

He frowned. "Just keep driving. I'll tell you as we go."

"You're Pharaoh's smuggling connection, aren't you? Or should I call him, Mr. Max Hoffman, double agent, mole, and Deputy Director of Operations for the Central Intelligence Agency?"

"You know somethin' kid? You're a nosey little puke. I can see why Hoffman wants you terminated. Go left up here."

"Here? You mean, head south on Capital Beltway?"

I sure hoped Cole was listening to this. And I prayed he wasn't in on it. One way or another, I'd find out soon enough. I jabbered away, narrating our progress like Agent Vern Bozowski had done on the bus.

Finally Sly cut me off. "Just shut your damn trap, kid."

"But, uh, I talk when I get nervous. With your gun in my ribs, I might make a mistake. We wouldn't want to have an accident, now would we?" Sly just scowled back, which I took to mean ok.

Sly pointed ahead. "Turn up here."

"Oh, at the Dulles Airport turnoff? So, the warehouse is at the airport, huh? And I bet Hoffman's already there in his blue Mercedes after he kidnapped Bob with it."

We reached the warehouse and circled around the building to the back. Sure enough, like a sentry guarding the black knight's castle, Hoffman's shiny blue ride sat by the entrance. I pulled up next to it.

Grabbing me by my jacket collar, Sly dragged me out and shoved me inside.

Darkness blinded me. As my eyes adjusted to the dim light, shadows formed into distinctive silhouettes. Crates of all sizes, stacked from floor to ceiling, littered the enormous warehouse floor. With his Glock at my back, Sly prodded me down a path between the boxes.

A thin beam of light shined from a clearing ahead. And there Hoffman stood, an Ingram submachine gun in hand. Bound tight to a chair, a piece of duct tape strapped over his mouth, sat Bob.

As we entered the clearing, Hoffman grinned.

"Ah, the Artful Dodger! I'm glad you could join us. You've proven to be a most worthy adversary. Congratulations! You lose."

Sly handed his Glock pistol to Hoffman. From the shadows, Sly grabbed a chair and a rope. Hoffman stuffed the handgun into his coat pocket.

"I'm afraid you bit off too much when your friend stole my wallet, Justin. Let that be a lesson. Never pick a pickpocket's pocket." He walked toward me. "I knew I was being set up. I let him take it. And plant the tracker bug. Trackers work both ways, Justin; I knew you'd stay close to me as well."

"So you're the Pharaoh, aren't you?"

"Yes. And no. I made him up. Created a phantom agent named Pharaoh to draw the heat from me when your father discovered my operation and reported it to CIA." He waved with a hand to Sly's chair. "Take a seat."

I did. Sly bound my wrists, each hand tied separately to either side of the chair.

"So, Hoffman, you're the one selling secrets to foreign spies through Sly's workers."

He shrugged. "Highest bidder takes all. Or at least the top two or three." He turned to Sly. "Cover the door. This won't take long."

Sly ran off. Hoffman pulled up a chair and sat backwards in it, facing Bob and me. He hung his hairy arms over the seat back and idly played with the Ingram in a very intimidating way. He looked deep into my eyes, his pupils like green spotlights shining on my deepest thoughts. "Now tell me, Justin, where is the key to *Rubber Soul*?"

I stared straight ahead. "I don't know what you're talking about."

He narrowed his eyes. "And your eyes say you do. Don't waste my time, Dodger. You've wasted enough already. I've waited *years* to get to this position in the CIA, so I could reopen your case and find the key before Cole did. But, just like your father, you never came up with it."

"And I won't. You'll never get your dirty millions."

"Millions? Hah! Try billions, Reed. *Billions.*"

The word took my breath away. "What in the world for?"

"What in the world for? Why, to buy the world, of course."

"You're a freakin' lunatic."

He smirked. "Crazy like a fox. Just like Hitler. And he nearly succeeded."

"What are you, a neo Nazi or something?"

He chuckled. "Oh, nothing so idealistic. Megalomaniac, you might call it." He thrust his face forward, eyes wild with delight. "Included in the selling price of each secret comes a piece of that country's operation. A drug lab here, a Mafia connection there. Soon, I'll control the drug cartels of of the Americas, Asia and the Middle East, and with them, their governments. And I'll be in charge of the CIA, the most powerful intelligence agency the world has ever known."

I shook my head. "In case you forgot, Hoffman, Cole's in line as the next Director, not you."

Hoffman shrugged. "Accidents are easy to arrange in this business. As you and Bob are about to find out."

At that, the smart-a came out of me. "And what's next, Hoffman, President? You'd never win. You're too ugly."

He frowned. "I'll ignore your cheap barb, Reed. Besides, I don't have to. I'll be the power behind the throne. The puppeteer, as it were. I'll be the most powerful man in the world, and no one will even know it. Call it the New World Order."

"Impossible."

"Really? Remember your spy classes, Dodger. The most powerful men in history controlled either the drug trade or the best espionage network. I'll have both. From there, its an easy step to—"

He paused as he spied Carlos's chain around my neck. He yanked it over my head and held it up. As the key twisted on the chain, he flashed his wizard's grin.

"Thank you, Artful Dodger. You've just changed the course of world history." He dropped the chain over his head and hefted the Ingram machine gun. He stood and walked around behind me.

I craned my neck to see him, but couldn't. For the second time that day, I felt the cold steel of a gun barrel dig into the flesh of my neck. I gulped and closed my eyes.

"Goodbye, Justin. Your country is grateful for your service."

"*Mmm,*" Bob mumbled excitedly from beneath his gag.

Hoffman said, "Yes, Mr. Cheney? You have something to contribute to this conversation?" He ripped the tape from Bob's mouth. I winced.

"Let the boy go, Hoffman. You're too late. I already told Cole who you are. Give it up."

"Don't give me that crap, Cheney. You didn't talk to Cole or anyone. You never once picked up your phone when I followed you to the mall. Besides, this provides me with the perfect solution. You kidnapped and shot Justin to keep him from exposing you." Hoffman hooked his machine gun back beneath his overcoat.

From atop a crate he picked up a rum bottle full of red liquid, a rag plugging its end. A Molotov cocktail, filled with gasoline. He ignited the rag with a lighter. The tiny flame flickered then blossomed as it consumed the dry cloth.

"Then you set fire to this warehouse to cover your crime. But you were too slow to escape, and perished in the flames."

He tossed the bomb across the room. The bottle smashed across a stack of crates. Fire leapt toward the ceiling. The flames quickly spread.

Hoffman sighed. "I hate to give up the valuable contents of this warehouse, but one must always be ready to cut losses. Besides, " he fingered the chain and key, "this is quite a satisfactory tradeoff."

The warehouse door burst open. I turned to see two figures rush in. One tackled Sly with the force and skill of a seasoned linebacker. My mouth dropped open as I recognized the attacker.

"Glen," I screamed.

Hoffman wheeled around in surprise. In that instant, Bob kicked at Hoffman's ankles. Hoffman fell.

Into the clearing the other figure raced, pistol in hand. Elation zapped me like an electric shock.

"Carlos!"

He waved with his gun. "How are you, kid?"

I had no clue how they'd found us, but this was no time for questions. "Watch it, Carlos, he's got a—"

Too late. Hoffman brought his Ingram around and fired a stream of bullets. Carlos dove behind a crate. Splinters exploded from his wooden shield. Hoffman jumped to his feet and sprinted for cover.

Carlos popped up behind another box and fired back. Just before Hoffman reached cover, a lucky bullet hit his hand. He screamed in pain. The machine gun clattered to the ground. He retreated to the back of the room. Carlos bolted after him.

"Careful, he's still got a pistol," I shouted. Carlos waved acknowledgment and disappeared into the darkness.

"How you doin', Justin?" Glen called.

"Great, now that you're here. How in the world did you guys find us?"

"Got your phone call."

"I called *you*?" I exclaimed. "I thought I'd hit CIA's speed dial."

"Get out of here, Glen," Bob shouted. "This isn't over yet."

"Oh, I can't move right now, Mr. Cheney. You see, I'm sitting on top of this megaloser I just tackled. Ugly as sin, too."

I had to laugh. "Take good care of that 'megaloser', Glen. He's the slimeball who killed my father."

"He's not going anywhere. I got him face down with his arm pinned behind his back. In fact, I think it deserves a good twist, now that I know who he is." Sly let out a yelp of pain that sounded like music to my ears.

A shot rang out from Carlos's pistol, followed by two from Hoffman's Glock. I clenched my teeth.

Smoke from the fire invaded my nostrils. I coughed.

Bob said, "Justin, scoot over here. My cuff link is a rasp saw. Can you reach it?"

"Yeah." I hopped the chair closer, then backed up to him and stretched my fingers out. I found his cuff link and yanked. It came off in my palm. I clasped it hard, and reached for his ropes. I sawed at his bindings, rotating my wrist back and forth like a rocker strumming his guitar.

Flames crept toward us. Heat from the inferno warmed my cheek. Sweat trickled down my forehead. Two more shots rang out, one from each gun, farther back in the warehouse. As long as Carlos kept firing, I knew he was still alive.

The fire robbed oxygen from the air. I gasped for breath.

"Almost done," I wheezed, cutting through the last strands of rope.

Bob yanked hard, and broke free. He quickly freed his other hand.

A clap of thunder pummeled my ears. The back of the warehouse erupted in an orange and yellow fireball.

"Carlos," I screamed. But the explosion drowned out my cry.

Bob leaped from his seat and tossed me, chair and all, to the ground. He covered me with his body. Debris rained down.

In the distraction of the explosion, Sly broke free and threw Glen to the ground. I gaped in horror as Sly stood over Glen and raised his switchblade.

"Bob, help," I stammered, pointing.

Bob lunged for the Ingram machine gun, whipped around and fired just as Sly thrust down. Sly recoiled against the wall and slumped to the ground. Glen rolled away unharmed.

Bob quickly untied me. Just as he finished, a figure emerged from the back, running fast toward us. Bob held up the Ingram, then relaxed. I breathed an enormous sigh of relief as Carlos ran up.

"We've got to get out of here," he said, breathless. "The whole warehouse is filled with ordnance."

"Did you get Hoffman?" Bob asked.

Carlos shrugged. "I'm a lousy shot, but I must've hit a box of grenades or something. I'd say he's vaporized."

We raced out. As we passed through the door, I slapped Glen on the back.

He grinned. "Nice blond hairdo, *Agent Shadow*."

I laughed. "It's *Dodger*, now."

"Hmph. You know, for a freshman, you're pretty cool. I guess you can date my sister."

I glanced at him. "No noggin' beaning?"

"No noggin' beaning."

"You're on!"

The two men dragged Sly across the street while Glen drove me in his Mustang away from the burning building. We pulled up next to Bob. Getting out, I looked down at Sly's body. My lips trembled.

"Is he . . . ."

"Dead."

I stared at the corpse of the man who'd killed my father. I'd always dreamed of this moment, but never thought the emotion running through me would be regret.

Bob laid a hand on my shoulder. "Hey. Better him than you." He turned to Carlos. "A warehouse full of military arms, hmm?"

As if on cue, an explosion ripped through the roof. Flames leapt skyward.

Carlos nodded. "Looks like."

"So, drugs and secrets weren't all that Hoffman smuggled," Bob said. "There's going to be quite an inquiry into this."

I straightened up. "Oh, um, Bob. Meet Carlos." They shook hands.

With a smirk Bob said, "I am *extremely* happy to make your acquaintance, sir. Your sense of timing is exemplary."

"No problem, *amigo*. I owe this boy's father my life."

I hugged Carlos and patted him on the back. "I knew you couldn't turn down a chance to get even. And Glen, that was the greatest tackle of your career. I owe you one. A big one."

We high-fived. "Hey, Justin, I just hope you teach your martial arts skills to our high school wrestling team this year."

I laughed and glanced at Bob. "Well, we'll see. Now tell me, guys, I'm dying to know. How did you find us?"

Glen shrugged. "When I got home from the funeral, I saw Carlos nosing around your house. So, I ran across the street and confronted him."

Carlos said, "I knew Bob would be at the funeral, so I took the opportunity to do some snooping."

Glen continued. "Right after that, your call from Bob's phone rang my cell. We jammed here as fast as we could."

Sirens whispered in the distance, then quickly swelled to a wail. Two cop cars screeched up first, red lights sparkling through the nighttime drizzle. Bob met them, flashed his CIA badge and explained the story. No doubt an altered version dreamed up just for them.

The scene turned to bedlam as fire trucks, ambulances and news vans all screamed up. Three FBI agents jumped from a car and flocked to Bob, who talked with them for several minutes.

We stood there for an hour or so, standing under an awning to avoid the drizzle, while firemen slowly brought the blaze under control.

Cole pulled up in his BMW. He stepped out. When he saw me, his eyes nearly bugged out of his head. He stormed toward me, but Bob intercepted. As Bob explained, Cole's expression changed from anger to surprise to joy. They talked a few more minutes, then Bob's face lit up as well. Cole marched over to me with his hand extended.

"Percival Brimley," he exclaimed. "You are a remarkable young man. Let me shake your hand."

He shook it, all right. Almost pulled my arm from my socket. He looked to Glen and Carlos, who were both trying desperately to stifle their snickers after hearing my hideous fake name. My glare burned holes in their brains.

"May we speak in private?" Cole asked.

The two glanced at each other.

"OK, *Percival*," Glen exclaimed. The two lost it then, bellowing and slapping each other on the back as they sauntered off.

Cole said, "You did what my entire intelligence force could not. You single-handedly broke the *Rubber Soul* smuggling ring and saved an agent's life. Bob tells me your spyPhone recorded Hoffman's confession of his guilt and Bob and your father's innocence."

I nodded.

Cole's eyes darted right and left, then he cleared his throat and bent closer. "It seems as though I owe you an apology. I confess, Hoffman talked me into using you to flush out the Pharaoh. I should have known better. Forgive my arrogance, and my ignorance at not seeing the real enemy. I . . . I guess I was desperate. The leaks had become an awful embarrassment to my department."

Cole straightened and looked down on me with pride, like a general presenting a medal to a soldier. "We have a place at the Company for resourceful young men like you. When you finish school, I'd like to offer you a position."

I stared into his eyes, a smile slowly spreading across my face. "Thanks, but no thanks. I'm too old for this sort of thing."

"Too old? Why, you're just a high school student."

"I know. I've had enough of your kids' game."

He laughed. "Kid's game? Well, I suppose you're right. It is rather childish for world governments to hide in each other's closets at night. But in today's imperfect world it still is a necessary evil, I'm afraid. Justin, your country truly is grateful for your service. There's a large reward for the capture of Pharaoh. Looks like you get it. And if there's anything else I can do to convince you to work for me, just name it."

I took a big breath. "Well, there are a couple of things that *might* make me reconsider . . . ."

"Such as?"

"I'm not saying I'm interested, understand. But I think you owe me."

"I most certainly do, son. What do you want?"

I laid it on him. "I want a new birth certificate. One with my real name, not this Percival Brimley crap."

"Hmm, I certainly understand. Very well." He scribbled the note on his pad then snapped the notebook shut.

"*And* . . . ."

He reopened it.

"There's a girl from Nicaragua named Mira Dominguez. She's living as an illegal alien in New York. I want her to receive full citizenship, no questions asked."

He scribbled, then started to close it again.

I held up a finger. "I want her whole family brought here, and their citizenships granted, compliments of the CIA. They could use jobs, too."

He placed a fist on his hip and smirked. "Is that *all*?"

"One more thing."

"Oh?"

"An orphan named Randy was sent to juvenile prison for confessing to a crime that I committed. I want him released, and his record wiped clean."

He sighed and thought a moment. "Hmm. That's a bit tricky, but I'll do my best."

"See that your best is good enough."

Cole chuckled and cast a glance at Bob. "Kid doesn't ask for much, does he?"

Bob waved a hand. "One thing I've learned from living with him. He's always known what he wants."

Cole wrote the last bit down. He tucked the note pad in his coat and looked up. "I'll try to get it all done before you leave for L.A."

I raised a brow. "L.A.? What do you mean by that?"

He shrugged. "Well, the mission's over, so you can't stay here with Bob. He'd have to quit the Company. You *do* want to live in the L.A. orphanage, don't you?"

I hadn't even thought of that. Now that Pharaoh was history, I had to leave Bob.

I looked at him. "So I guess this is goodbye?"

Bob's eyes darted between Cole and me. He grabbed my shoulders and bent closer. "Listen, Justin. Mr. Cole just promoted me to Senior Counterintelligence Specialist. That means I coordinate covert field operations, and participate in them as necessary. It's a huge promotion."

"Congratulations," I mumbled.

"I can do so much for the country now. The CIA's getting fully involved in the drug war. For you and me, it's payback time. I could cripple the drug trade like never before. Think of it."

I did. I had just broken an entire cocaine smuggling ring and avenged my father's death. But the victory somehow rang hollow.

From behind the police barriers, TV floodlights blasted us. Cole said, "You and Bob better scram. We can't have our future top agent on the nine o'clock news."

We slipped into the darkness while Cole confronted the reporters.

Bob spoke. "You'll get everything. I'll see to it myself."

I stopped and turned. "Everything? All I really ever wanted was to go fishing. Fishing with Dad."

"But you're dad's gone, Justin."

I stared at him, long and hard. "Yeah. Yeah, I guess he is."

Running a hand through his hair, he sighed. "Look, Justin. If you stayed here with me, how would your life be, hmm? With me gone all the time, running all over the world chasing drug smugglers, terrorists, and who knows what scum, and you knowing the torturous secret of my dual existence? You deserve better than that. I'd have to quit the Company, like Cole said."

"Forget it." I swept my hand in dismissal then walked away. I joined Carlos and Glen. Bob followed at my heels.

Putting a hand on Carlos's back, I flashed an annoyed glance at Bob. "Carlos, could I crash with you tonight? I once again find myself an orphan."

"Of course."

I turned to Glen. "And how 'bout giving us a ride?"

"Uh, sure," he said, his eyes darting between Bob and me.

"Later, Mr. Chanley," I called behind my back, mispronouncing it like I had when we first met. "I'll be by tomorrow to collect my stuff."

He stared back, unable to speak.

CHAPTER 12: L.A.

I stayed a few extra days to debrief. During that time, CIA rounded up Scarface and the rest of Hoffman's henchmen. In the files of the official investigation, CIA completely cleared my father's name, crediting Agent Blue Jay with discovering the *Rubber Soul* Op. Credit for breaking the case went to Bob, and a mythical CIA agent named the Artful Dodger. I was listed as a "witness."

I promised Joya I'd call her as soon as I hit L.A. She hit my arm in reply. Rubbing my sore bicep, I knew it was her version of a goodbye kiss.

Glen drove me up to the orphanage to say goodbye to the gang, including Randy, out of Juvy for good. And I saw Mrs. Kraumas, who hugged me forever, her tears flooding the building.

I saw Mira one last time. She received a nice chunk of change for her help, which she said she'd use to start a new life in America, the way she and her sister had originally intended.

For his part, Carlos received a huge reward. He planned to move his family out of the barrio and enroll in electrician's school.

I only saw Bob once, when I went to collect my stuff at his house. He wished me good luck, and presented me with a gift, the Colt Pocketlite pistol I'd trained with. I didn't much care to have a gun lying around, but he insisted that I'd need it in the "big city of L.A." Reluctantly, I accepted.

He didn't ask me to stay, and I didn't suggest it.

I didn't care any more.

Cole gave me a new birth certificate with my real name, but with the fake age of eighteen. And the promise of a spy job when I was ready. Yeah, right.

I used a huge chunk of my reward money to buy *Shadow*, the hot Camaro I'd trained with; most of the rest of the dough was donated to the North Brooklyn Orphanage by one "Percival Brimley." I wasn't due to check into the L.A. orphanage for a week, which gave me time to drive *Shadow* cross-country. The only orphan in L.A. who owned his own car. Or was a CIA-trained spy, for that matter.

I started out.

Once past the toll booth and on the Jersey Turnpike, I hit the throttle. Light poles whizzed by. Wind whipped my face. With the windows open it sounded like a jet. I zoomed past the other cars, zigzagging between lanes.

I said to myself, "I'm free. No one's hounding me. I could go anywhere, do anything, be anyone. And, I don't have to worry about where my next meal's coming from."

I recalled how thrilled I felt the first time I rode in Bob's Vette.

"Who needs him?" I mumbled, wiping away a tear.

I reached L.A., and drove straight to my parents' cemetery. I sat cross-legged on the cool grass that carpeted their graves.

From my backpack, I pulled out the pistol and curled my fingers around it one last time. The gun felt comfortable in my palm. Too comfortable.

Thoughts of the events that led me here ran through my mind; the baseball game, the bus escape, the New York mission. My funeral.

I sat with Mom and Dad all afternoon, all evening, the sun setting, darkness falling. Beams from the half moon pierced the foliage and broke my trance.

With fingernails, I clawed the earth from the base of Dad's tombstone. The damp soil pulled away easily.

"I lived for awhile by the sword, Dad, and like you I learned the hard way. But I'm burying it now. The sword, the hatchet, the gun. Right here, right where you can watch it, and keep it away from me."

I set the gun in the hole, covered it over and patted the soil.

"I'll make it to college, Dad, I promise. I know what I want to be now."

Sitting back, I surveyed my parents' graves, and the smaller one containing the pistol. With these three mounds, I buried my two pasts. I brushed the dirt from my palms and stood.

"I'll join you some day, Mom and Dad. But it won't be soon."

"Sooner than you think, Dodger."

I jumped and turned in surprise. I spied a man lurking in the shadows of an elm. I couldn't see his face, but his raspy voice I knew too well.

"*Pharaoh!*"

I thought I'd shouted his name, but all that came from me was a whisper.

"It's about time you got rid of that damned gun."

Out of the shadows, he stepped toward me.

Then I saw his face, disfigured from the warehouse explosion. I gasped in horror. His left eye was swollen shut in blue black, pussed and wrinkled skin. A scar creased his left cheek and pulled his lips down into a lopsided frown. His left hand, injured from Carlos's bullet, hung in a sling. Then I saw the Glock pistol leveled at me from his right hand.

I froze, unable to move, to think, to breathe.

"How did you—"

"Survive, Justin? There's more than one way out of a building. Didn't you ever read about trap doors and secret passageways in your little spy classes?" He limped forward. "Or do you mean, how did I find you? Quite simple really, where else would you go? Stupid, Reed. You left the protective bosom of the Company before you knew what happened to me. Your father would be disappointed at your foolishness. Runs in the family, I guess."

He edged closer. I glanced right and left, looking for a place to run, to hide.

"Oh, no, Artful Dodger, you can't dodge me now. And no one can hear your screams. I took out the night guard an hour ago. But don't worry. I'm here to give you what you dearly want most. I'm going to send you to see your parents."

"N-no." I backed away. I bumped into Mom's headstone.

"But first, tell me the account number. See, when you destroyed my CIA career, I also lost clearance to the account's access number. But I still have the key. So what is the number?"

"I-I don't know. I swear it."

"*Chiyaa!*" A roundhouse kick struck my face and knocked me backward over the grave marker.

"That's for Sly."

The kick stunned me, but training took over. I somersaulted backward and stood. Another blow sent me tumbling to the ground. I don't know whether it had been from a fist or a foot, but it bloodied my nose.

"That's for my career."

I lay on my hands and knees, unable to escape.

"Come on, Reed. The number's no good to you now. Except to buy you a quick death with much, *much* less pain. Let me refresh your memory. The number starts, 'Six-four-three'. What is the rest?"

I closed my lips tight and breathed through my nostrils like a winded horse.

"Still don't remember? Maybe this will jar it loose."

He grabbed the back of my belt, lifted, and threw me head first into Dad's gravestone. Streaks of light darted about my eyes. I fell to the ground, panting. Dirt and blood mixed on my tongue and filled my nostrils. I choked and coughed. Grit crunched between my teeth.

"That was for destroying *Rubber Soul*. And this"—I heard two quick clicks, the unique sound of a silencer locking into place—"is for me."

I craned my stiff neck around. My left eye was swollen shut, like his. My whole sight was bathed in red, from the blood vessels swelled up inside my eyeball.

His blurry figure towered over me, lit in small patches of moonbeam. His one eye, open wide in rage, stared down, round and aglow like a second moon. He cocked the pistol and leveled it at me.

"One last time, Reed. What is the number?"

I turned away and looked at Dad's grave marker, inches in front of my eyes. "Dad, if you can help me—"

Then I saw it.

There, at the base of the marker, etched in stone and glowing fluorescent silver in the moonlight, a tiny line of numbers shone:

6-4-3 . . .

I gasped. The words from Dad's letter echoed in my ears.

Come visit me, and I shall give you the key to Rubber Soul.

Hoffman yanked me aside and read the numbers.

"Why, Master Reed! How ingenious. If a bit morbid. No wonder you were in such a rush to get here. You know, I almost started to believe that you really knew nothing. Congratulations, my friend, your ingenuity has earned you a relatively quick and painless death."

I rolled onto my back. He stood over me. His insane, uneven frown twisted into his wizard's smile. He raised the pistol high above his head, then, ever so slowly, lowered it down, down to take careful aim at my skull. My muscles went limp. I closed my eyes.

"*Pharaoh,*" a distant voice yelled.

Hoffman wheeled in surprise and fired wildly down the hill.

Gathering all my strength, I drew up my feet and kicked. Into his groin.

"*Aghh,*" Hoffman shrieked. He doubled over and fell to the ground. I scrambled out of reach.

I dug at Dad's grave—and the freshly buried handgun.

Hoffman moaned. I glanced back. He rolled to his knees and glared. His hunter's eye burned into me as if a target was tattooed to my forehead. He raised his pistol and aimed.

A figure leapt from the bushes. His body slammed Hoffman's into the side of a granite crypt. The blow knocked Hoffman's pistol to the ground. Then I recognized the attacker, and realized who had shouted from below.

"Bob," I cried.

The foes rebounded and staggered back to face each other. Bob struck two quick blows to Hoffman's stomach, then an uppercut to his chin. Hoffman's head snapped back into the stone wall. Hoffman shook his head, leaned against the crypt wall and kicked Bob's chest. Bob flew backward. I winced as his head struck the edge of a tombstone. He lay motionless, sprawled on the lawn.

Hoffman searched the shadows for his Glock.

I clawed frantically at the dirt.

Hoffman grabbed his pistol. I wrenched the Colt from its grave, spun and aimed.

Adrenaline kicked my brain into high gear. Time slowed. At this range, I knew, I could shoot Hoffman through the heart. Shoot to kill. That's what CIA had drilled into me, time and time again.

But I had another choice.

I had a split second to choose, but knew the decision would stay with me for the rest of my life.

I fired.

The gun kicked in my hands. The report deafened my ears. The muzzle flash burned streaks into my retinas. Squinting, I snapped the weapon back on target.

Hoffman recoiled into the crypt wall. Blood from his arm wound streaked across the monolith. He aimed once more. I fired again. His arm snapped back. He moaned, and breathed in deep, heavy gales as he transferred the pistol to his sling hand. He aimed. Again I fired. And again. With each shot, his body jerked and danced along the crypt wall like a marionette.

He went limp. The gun dropped from his hand. He slid to the ground, smearing a black trail of blood along the stone.

I leaned back against Dad's marker. The gun slipped from my fingers. What strength was left drained away. My stomach churned. I bent over and vomited.

When I sat back up, warm blood dribbled down my chin and splashed to my chest. I held a hand to my nostrils.

I looked back at the latest ghoul to haunt this cemetery. The great and evil Max Hoffman, alias the Pharaoh, smuggler, spy, traitor, lay helpless and dying in a pool of his own blood.

What a sight we made, pale, bloody, bruised and battered. If some kids had crashed the graveyard in search of midnight kicks right then, we'd have scared them to death for sure.

Bob groaned. Holding his head, he sat upright. He spotted Hoffman, then looked to me. I nodded.

He smiled. I didn't return the expression.

He shook his head in disbelief. "Well, you're a sorry sight. You okay?"

"Why didn't you have your gun?"

He held a palm out. "I didn't know I'd find you here, let alone him." He scrambled over to Hoffman and checked for a pulse.

I held my breath. "Is he . . . ?"

"Alive," he announced. "You managed to shoot just about every limb he's got, but he's still kicking. Figuratively, that is."

I breathed a huge sigh of relief, then lay back and rested. Bob quickly ripped his shirt into makeshift tourniquets, which he bound around Pharaoh's wounds. He stood and slapped his hands. "Good for now. At least he won't bleed to death." Limping toward me, Bob pulled out his spyPhone and made a quick call to 911. Hanging up, he knelt down before me. "Let's take a look at that nose, shall we?" He reached for my face like an all-knowing doctor.

I jerked away from his hand. I sniffed, and not just from the blood. "I don't need your help any more. We're even. I saved your life, you saved mine. Now get out of mine."

He pulled back. I pushed to my feet and staggered away. With my back to him, he couldn't see the tears welling up.

I stooped over Hoffman and removed my gold chain and key from his neck, then tossed one last insult Bob's way.

"Cheney, as far as I'm concerned, none of this ever happened. As you spooks are so fond of saying."

Softly, he said, "Come back with me, Justin."

I bounded down the hill. He followed.

Over my shoulder I said, "Why? You want to use me for another mission? One I have to accomplish or the world will fall apart?"

"As a matter of fact I do have a mission for you, a big one. The toughest assignment you'll ever face. The mission of being my son."

I stopped, but didn't turn.

"And yes, Justin, if you don't accomplish it, the world will fall apart. My world."

I cocked my head and looked sideways at him. "Don't snow me Bob."

"I've applied to adopt you, Justin. Here are the documents." He pulled a rolled up bundle of papers from his inside pocket. "They're a bit ragged from the fight, but everything's in order." He paused, glanced at his feet, then looked me square in the eye. "I quit the Company."

"You-you did?"

"It's all behind me, Justin. Well, almost. Basically, if my superior and I agree, I can get out on three weeks' notice." With a grin, he nodded back up the hill toward Hoffman. "I think my 'superior' won't put up much of a fuss." We both laughed at that. "Look, Justin, I've wanted you to stay with me all along. But I felt . . . guilty. Guilty that you were becoming a substitute for Eddie. That maybe I was betraying his memory by letting you in."

"Bob, a person adopts because of love for that person. Not because something is missing from his life. I wanted a father. Since Dad was gone, I didn't feel guilty being with you. I knew Dad would want it that way."

"And that's a wise attitude, Justin, one that took me months to learn. As a psychologist I should have known better. But sitting at home alone these last few days, feeling the house empty once again, just like after Eddie died, I did a lot of thinking. And learning about myself. Couldn't admit it before, but now I realize that's why I volunteered to be your guardian, why I even considered Cole and Hoffman's absurd plan in the first place. Not just to protect you from Pharaoh, but to make you my son. Now I realize Hoffman had manipulated my grief for his own ends. He really was crazy like a fox." He shrugged, and lightened his tone. "So, now that I've got a family again, I don't need to volunteer for any more suicide missions, right?"

"N-no, I guess not."

"So how about it? Father and son. No spy business. Deal?"

"Deal!" I shook his hand. Then hugged him, a great, big bear hug.

He slapped my back and chuckled. "Actually, you're a lot like Eddie. Feisty, independent, intelligent. With an *uncanny* knack for finding trouble."

I rolled my eyes. "That's me, the Artful Dodger."

He rubbed his hands together. "You know, most of my three weeks left with the Company I can spend in accrued vacation. So, I thought, since we're here in California, a nice, long fishing trip in the Sierras sounded good."

I snapped my fingers. "I know just the place."

"Of course, we'll have to buy all new camping gear. I didn't bring anything. Not that I'm broke, mind you, but I'm practically unemployed." He winked.

It was my turn to look back up the hill and grin. "Oh, I don't think money will be a problem anytime soon."

He raised his brows. *Later*, I was about to say, when distant sirens pierced the graveyard silence.

I sighed. "Here we go again."

He glanced at his watch. "It's about time. Look, I'll handle this. You keep a low profile in the *Shadow*. The 'Intels' should be right behind," he finished, referring to the FBI, CIA, NSA and the like.

"Say, what about the cemetery guard?"

"He's okay. Nasty concussion, though."

"Thank God. I figured him a goner."

We stepped through the cemetery gate and made for the parking lot, walking side by side.

I looked up at him. "So, what are you going to do, now that you're retiring? Become a bum? Add to our homeless problem?"

He shook his head. "I've always wanted to finish my doctorate and go into private practice. With a twinkle in his eye, he said, "Hey, maybe help 'environmentally challenged juveniles' like yourself." We laughed. He said, "You know, I just realized that I've never asked what you want to be when you grow up. Not a spy, I know, though Cole will be disappointed. What then? What else is there to life?"

"I never knew. But now I've decided on something nice and quiet."

"Such as?"

"High school P.E. teacher."

He snapped his head back and cackled. "Are you kidding? A class full of rowdy freshmen will make Pharaoh look like the Pope. Besides, you have to get through high school as a *student*, first."

We strolled out to *Shadow*.

I sighed. "You know, the spy business wasn't all that bad. The excitement . . . ."

"The adventure," he added.

"The glamour."

"Women falling at your feet." We chuckled, then he looked at me with raised eyebrows. "Having second thoughts?"

"Who, me?" I curled my lips, as if faced with a dilemma. "Give me a few days fishin' and I'll get back to you on that."

I could already taste the trout, fried up nice and fresh on the camp stove by Dad—

I mean, Bob.

The End

Special request by the Author:
Please leave an honest rating and review of this book, to help others decide whether to read it. U.S. Amazon Link: amazon.com/author/ericauxier

AFTERWARD: BE A HERO

Justin Reed, aka The Artful Dodger, is a fictional character. Through his adventures, we get to solve the world's problems.

But the reality is, problems are not so easily solved.

If you or someone you know is involved with a gang, or is a victim of any form of crime, be a hero like Justin and contact one of these organizations:

Report a Crime/Tip Line

- **Report a Crime:**
  http://www.justice.gov/actioncenter/report-crime
- **DEA Drug Tip Line**: 877-RxAbuse (877-792-2873)
- **FBI Tip Reporting**: https://tips.fbi.gov
- **National Gang Center**:
  https://www.nationalgangcenter.gov

Drugs/Mental Health/Seek Help

- **SAMHSA—(Drugs/Mental Health Help):**
  1-800-662-HELP (4357); http://www.samhsa.gov
- **Suicide Prevention Hotline:** 1-800-273-TALK (8255)
- **Bullying/Cyber Bullying:** http://www.stopbullying.gov

A portion of proceeds from the author's books go to the international orphan charities:
- warmblankets.org
- flyingkites.org

ALSO BY THE AUTHOR

If you enjoyed **Mission 1: Operation** Rubber Soul,
check out Justin's other missions!
Missions are episodic, and can be read in any order

CODE NAME: DODGER SPY/FLY SERIES

Mission 2: Cartel Kidnapping

*"Who is the great CIA Agent, Artful Dodger? Tell me now,
and I kill you quick."*

Bob is kidnapped, and Justin tracks his newly-adopted father to a top secret smuggling base, where he is forced to match wits with a cartel family's brilliant teen prodigy, Luis Ocho.

But Luis's stunning teen sister Kiara is another story. Is she falling for Justin, or is this just another one of Luis's diabolical tricks to lure the "great Agent Dodger" to his demise? Once again, Justin must rely on his old street smarts—and his new CIA training—to face a ruthless and deadly enemy.

TOP SECRET
EYES ONLY

TO: KING COLE/CIA HQ
FR: AGENT ANACONDA
LOC: CUIDAD JUAREZ, MEXICO
OP: RATTLESNAKE
DRUG LORD ESTEBAN OCHO HAS DISPATCHED TOP AGENTS TO U.S.
SUSPECT RETALIATION AGAINST AGENTS FAGIN AND ARTFUL DODGER
FOR DESTROYING OCHO/PHARAOH SMUGGLING RING.
IMMEDIATE ACTION REQD TO ENSURE THEIR SAFETY.
END MSG.

Cartel Kidnapping—Excerpt

"No more trouble, or I shoot you both," Pablo warned.

He sat us down on a log in the middle of camp. A henchman held an uzi machine gun to our backs.

Pablo reached into his satchel and pulled out a walkie-talkie. He held it to his lips and spoke, turning from us as he did. He announced in Spanish, "Conquistador, this is Fisherman. We have Agent Fagin and his boy. Proceed inbound for extraction. These GPS coordinates."

Luis barked to the others, "You two, come up the hill with me. We must clear a landing site." Everyone left but Pablo and the guard at our back.

I looked questioningly at Bob. With his eyes he motioned to his lap, directing my attention to his bound hands. One covered the other so that only I could see his fingers. Slowly, silently, he "spoke" in deaf sign language, forming letters with his fingers. I had learned some basic sign during CIA communications training, so I easily read his message: "Pharaoh's Mexican contacts," he spelled.

I tensed at the mention of Pharaoh. "Smugglers?" I asked with my hands. He nodded.

"What do they want?" I signed back.

"Revenge." A chill zapped down my spine.

Pablo turned and faced us.

"We have plane coming." I raised my brows. I knew he meant "helicopter," but I didn't bother correcting him. He who holds the gun is always right.

Playing with his huge knife, Pablo slowly circled us. Each time he went behind, it was all I could do to keep breathing. At any moment, I expected the blade to be thrust through my back.

Finally, Pablo crouched down before Bob. Slowly, menacingly, he played the buck knife across Bob's cheeks, as if giving him a shave.

"So tell me, Agent *Fagin*," he began, using Bob's top secret CIA code name. "Who is this great CIA Agent *Artful Dodger*?"

I bit my tongue, trying my best not to react. Bob stiffened, and tightened his lips.

"Tell me now, and we save much time. You die fast, no pain. I might even let de little boy go free. Minus a finger for a souvenir, hehehe." He slid the knife up and down Bob's throat. Bob flinched as the knife bit into his skin, drawing a trickle of blood. "I know he must be biiig boss man to bring down the great spy Pharaoh. So big, there is no CIA record. He not even exist. So I know. He big, big boss man. So I ask: who is the great Artful Dodger? And what does he know about the Ocho organization, hmm?" Bob stared straight ahead in defiance.

I wondered what Pablo would do if Bob told him the truth, that "the great Artful Dodger" was sitting right next to him. A scrawny little orphan kid with hardly two cents to his name. Probably laugh his head off, then take ours.

"Nothing to say?" Pablo asked. "*Gato* got your tongue?" He scooted over to squat before me. "Maybe I give de little boy a deep shave and we find out muuuch quicker, hmm?"

I gasped.

"Pablo!" Luis shouted.

Letting out an annoyed sigh, Pablo closed his eyes. "*Qué?*" he answered without turning.

"Papa will take care of the interrogation," Luis demanded in a sharp, angry voice.

"You're the boss," Pablo said, motioning for Bob and me to stand. We obediently followed him up the hill. The guard remained at our backs, machine gun ready.

The other guards scattered about, frantically tossing debris from a clearing between the tall pines. Luis directed the work at the makeshift landing pad. As we passed by, Luis took over for the guard. He shoved me forward. I stumbled, but recovered.

"Halt," he commanded.

We stopped. And waited. The workers finished their chore, and all was silent except for the rustle of pine and the crow of black ravens. After a few minutes, a new sound floated in on the breeze. I looked west through the pine tops and down the canyon, and could just make out a speck in the sky. The *whop-whop* grew louder and echoed through the canyon. Sunlight flashed off the rotors as the speck formed into the shape of a helicopter. I wished for a U.S. Forest Service chopper or, better yet, a CIA bird. But that was hopeless. Nobody but these guys knew our whereabouts. And how they found us, I hadn't a clue.

Pablo yelled instructions into his radio as the bird approached. I shut my eyes against the blast of dust as the chopper circled overhead, sizing up the landing area. He finally decided to come up the river and through a cut in the trees next to camp. The craft settled onto the bed of soft earth, green ferns and dry pine needles in front of us. Luis shoved me again, and the force knocked me to the ground. I glared back at him.

Bob quickly pulled me to my feet. His gaze caught mine. "*Ato de,*" he said, speaking Japanese so only I could understand: "Later."

"*Silencio!*" Luis shouted above the din of churning rotor blades. "No talking. Get in." Luis prodded us onto the six seat chopper, boarding behind us. I sat in the far corner from the door, facing rearward, with Bob next to me. Pablo took an empty seat opposite us. Luis slammed the door shut and threw himself in the seat opposite me. Enraged, his eyes burned into mine. I lowered my head, and sobered up to the desperate situation Bob and I were in.

Revenge, I thought to myself. They—*he*—wants revenge.

A guard squeezed in and sat by the door, next to Bob. By the guy's wide eyes and tense muscles, I could tell he'd never been in a helicopter before. Neither had I, but I'd flown a lot. The guard leveled a shaky pistol at us and clutched the arm rest with his other hand.

The whine of the turbine engines increased and the rotor blades began to whirl at blinding speed. My guts sank as the helicopter lifted.

The guard stiffened and whimpered, clutching tighter at the arm rest. He stared longingly out the window in the door. I traded glances with Bob; he'd noticed the guard's distraction too.

If there was just some way to break free, and hide from the goons on the ground . . . .

Any escape had to come now. Right now.

The pilot gingerly floated the craft between the trees and out over the rushing river. We inched along downstream toward the pool next to camp. Only ten feet above the water, I figured. If we could just jump out and hide somewhere. I had an idea.

I coughed loudly to get Bob's attention, then nodded to my lap. My hands were still bound at the wrists, so I covered one hand with the other and slowly signed the word, "R-I-V-E-R." I ended by pointing a thumb out the window. Instantly my adopted father/CIA trainer caught my meaning. He signaled back a countdown by slowly retracting each finger on one hand: 5-4-3-2-1.

Bob exploded into action. He elbowed the guard in the chin then launched his entire body at Luis and Pablo. I lunged for the door and popped it open, then dove outside.

I fell. And fell.

Impact.

"4 OUT OF 4 STARS! Fast-paced, action-packed spy novel. Grabs the reader hook, line, and sinker. Reluctant and avid readers who enjoy teenage fast-paced, spy adventure will love reading this book."
—Online Book Club

"Like Harry Potter, *this YA series is fun for kids of all ages!"*
—Tawni Waters, author, *Beauty of the Broken*

Mission 3: jihadi hijacking

Justin has settled into the quiet suburban life as secret agent Bob Cheney's newly-adopted son. Finally, he's put the nightmare of the spy world behind him for good. Or has he?

When their airliner is hijacked by armed terrorists—including a mysterious teen girl with striking green eyes—it's up to Justin and Bob to take it back. But that's only half the problem: even if they can overcome the terrorists, who's left to fly the plane?

Yet again, Justin must rely on his old orphan street smarts—and new CIA training—to take on armed terrorists and prevent apocalypse.

> *"4 OUT OF 4 STARS! Superb on so many levels. A highly detailed, entertaining, and character-driven spy thriller!"*
> —Online Book Club
> *"A free-wheeling, engaging espionage tale that aims to enlighten readers!"*—Kirkus Review

Mission 4: YAKUZA DYNASTY

"ONE OF THE BEST BOOKS I'VE EVER READ!
Absolutely in the same league as Harry Potter!"
—Online Book Club Official Review

The Artful Dodger faces his greatest foe yet: Himself!

Troubled by confusing childhood memories, Justin and his adopted secret agent father Bob search for clues to Justin's past. But his past, they discover too late, is searching for him.

Lost in Asia and inexplicably pursued by Korean and Japanese mobsters, Justin must use every ounce of his street skills and CIA training to battle mafia thugs, modern-day ninjas—and a stunning, pink-haired *harajuku* punker named Michiko.

Fighting for his very life, Justin unearths a secret from his childhood so shocking that not even his CIA training could prepare him.

FINAL MISSION
OF THE
CODE NAME: DODGER SPY/FLY SERIES!

THERE I WUZ!
ADVENTURES FROM 3 DECADES IN THE SKY—VOLUMES I-III

True tales from the author's life as an airline pilot!

"Captain, we've got a passenger losing consciousness."

What do you do, Captain?

In an Airbus A321 airliner traveling Mach .8, events come at you at ten miles a minute. As Captain, you must make sound decisions, using imperfect information and limited time. Nearly every decision is not black and white, but each is critical, has consequences.

Now, you are Captain. You get to call the shots, feel the urgency, the burden of command.

And you must make the right decisions that result in a safe, successful outcome.

Whether you are a seasoned warrior of the sky, fledgeling pilot about to embark on your own lifetime of adventures, or a "chairborne" avgeek, I invite you to explore this three part series. Just sit back, relax (well, as best you can, some of these stories are pretty hairy) and enjoy the ride!

THE LAST BUSH PILOTS

"Mayday, mayday, I'm going down!"

The frantic radio call rang in DC Alva's earphones. Instantly he recognized the pilot's voice: his best friend Allen Foley.

"Engine failure, south of Davidson Glacier," Allen's transmission continued. Then fell silent.

DC's guts churned. The glacier, the young pilot knew, was miles from civilization—and help. Worse, flying visually beneath the clouds as all Alaska bush pilots did, Allen would have mere seconds to save the plane.

Shoving the throttle full forward, DC banked his floatplane hard left, north up the coastline toward the crash site. The engine surged. The manifold pressure needle straddled red line. He crowded the rugged slopes of the Chilkat Range. Pine trees dense as shag carpet loomed below. *Taku* winds tumbled like whitewater over the cliffs and pummeled his craft. Left hand gripped tight about the control yoke and right hand working the throttle, he fought to keep the aircraft upright.

With trembling voice, DC relayed the distress call to headquarters. "SEAS Base, this is *Sitka Shrike*," he radioed, using the company's designated call sign for his plane. "*Gastineau King* just called, 'Mayday.' Engine's failed. South of Davidson. I'm enroute now."

Another crash, DC thought. One was seven times more likely to be struck by lightning, for God's sake. But once again, lightning had struck too close. The question burning in the back of his mind always was, Who next? Only in his darkest nightmares had he imagined . . .

Allen would be down by now. Images flashed through DC's mind of the man dying beneath a smoldering wreck. Instinctively he shoved again on the throttle, already firewalled.

"*Shrike* to *King*, do you read?" DC called. No reply. "*King*, this is *Shrike*, come in!" Static.

DC leaned over the controls and squinted through the plexiglass. Drizzle cut his view up the channel to a myopic three miles. Each visual cue, each bulge in the land or curve in the shore, floated toward him through the misty curtain like ghosts in a fog-shrouded graveyard.

"Coastline. Got to keep the coastline in sight," DC mumbled, not realizing he'd voiced the thought aloud. The leaden sky pressed down on him like the slab roof of a tomb. And it might as well be made of cement, he thought: fly into it, or penetrate the blinding rain ahead, and splat across the first mountain that came along. The moist air pressed through the cabin's filters and cooled his cheeks. He shivered, more from fear than chill. The drizzle turned to rain and formed a wall around him. The drops pelted his windshield. With each moment, the terrain popped through the curtain ever closer—visibility dropping fast. Less than a mile, he figured.

He cursed, throttling back. For Allen, every minute lost was a mile closer to death. But in this weather, speed was DC's first enemy. Any worse, and he would have to turn back or land.

The de Havilland Beaver floatplane slowed. As the airspeed trickled down, DC lowered a section of flaps to compensate. The trailing edge of the wings extended downward, adding lift.

He eyed the waves near shore. Chop the size of Volkswagens.

Even landing with engine power, he could dig a float or catch a wing and flip.

DC grimaced. Allen, flying a wheel plane, had even less hope. High tide covered the soft beach. Ocean waves slammed against a rocky shoreline, backed by a forest wall. Nowhere could he have glided to safety.

"*Shrike* to *King*, do you read?" DC called, for the hundredth time it seemed. "*King*, come in. At least key the mike!" No reply. "SEAS Base, what about rescue?"

"Coast Guard chopper's launched, ETA thirty minutes," the dispatcher's voice crackled.

"Can you make it through?" another pilot asked.

He eyed the wall of water ahead. "I—I'm not sure."

"Negative, *Shrike*," his Chief Pilot's voice cut in. "Weather's too solid. Seas are too rough for you, DC. Turn back."

But he couldn't shake the image of the dying man from his mind. He pressed on, squeezed between cloud and ground.

An hour passed—or a minute, he couldn't tell.

The drenched air formed fog; all turned murky. Forest, beach, even the air itself retreated into shadows of twilight. The saturated atmosphere phased between the elements of cloud and sky, water and air.

"Holy—" his voice trailed off. His gut churned. He'd heard of the phenomenon but had never seen it; never believed it could happen.

The sky fell.

The cloud base dropped, sucking the air below into its fold.

DC pushed forward on the yoke. The plane dove. He led the plummeting ceiling by a mere wingspan. The altimeter needle spun through five hundred feet.

Below the legal limit, he thought. But FAA rules were the least of his worries.

Four hundred . . three hundred . . the needle spiraled downward.

A glance out the side window: treetops whizzed by, inches below his floats. A startled eagle took wing.

"*Shrike*, I say again. Turn back immediately," his Chief Pilot ordered.

But his life's in my hands, he thought.

His hands. He looked at them, tight and trembling about the controls.

Flying through this weather was hazardous at best.

Flying through this weather could mean two accidents.

Flying through this weather would take all the training and all the experience he'd strived to gain while flying the Alaska bush—which, he realized now, was pitifully little.

If he crashed, his dream of flying for the airlines would crash too.

If he survived.

DC swallowed hard.

And made the toughest decision of his life.

Now in Print or Ebook at:
amazon.com/author/ericauxier

ABOUT THE AUTHOR
CODE NAME: FLYBOY

Captain Eric Auxier is a pilot by day, writer by night, and kid by choice.

Never one to believe in working for a living, his past list of occupations include: Alaska bush pilot, freelance writer, mural artist, blogger, and pilot for a Caribbean seaplane operation. He is now a Captain for a major U.S. airline.

Mr. Auxier has contributed to such publications as *Arizona Highways, Airways, Plane & Pilot* and *AOPA Pilot*. He is a graduate of Arizona State University (B.S. degree in Aeronautical Technology) and Cochise College (A.S. degree in Pro-Pilot). At both institutions, he worked as a newspaper editor, staff reporter and columnist.

The award-winning *Code Name: Dodger* is his first novel. His second, *The Last Bush Pilots*, captured the coveted **Amazon Top 100 Breakthrough Novel Awards** in 2013, and is an aviation techno-thriller based on his experience flying the Alaska bush. He is currently working on two new books, Volume II of *There I Wuz! Adventures From 3 Decades in the Sky*, and *Jihadi Hijacking*, Book 3 in the *Code Name: Dodger* adventure series.

Father of two, Mr. Auxier makes his home in Phoenix, Arizona.

A portion of proceeds from the author's books go to the international orphan relief funds, flyingkitesglobal.org and Warmblankets.org

CONTACT INFO:
AUTHOR BLOG: www.capnaux.com
CONTACT THE AUTHOR: Eric@capnaux.com
AUTHOR BOOK LINK: amazon.com/author/ericauxier

Made in the USA
Monee, IL
02 December 2023

48019400R00127